Cornelia Louisa Tuthill

Our Little Comfort

Fourth Edition

Cornelia Louisa Tuthill

Our Little Comfort
Fourth Edition

ISBN/EAN: 9783337266912

Printed in Europe, USA, Canada, Australia, Japan

Cover: Foto ©Andreas Hilbeck / pixelio.de

More available books at **www.hansebooks.com**

OUR LITTLE COMFORT.

N. ORR N.Y.

OUR LITTLE COMFORT.

By the Author of

"WREATHS AND BRANCHES FOR THE CHURCH;"
"CONSECRATED TALENTS;" ETC.

Blessed are the pure in heart; for they shall see God."

Fourth Edition.

NEW YORK:

GENERAL PROTESTANT EPISCOPAL S. S. UNION
AND CHURCH BOOK SOCIETY,

762 BROADWAY.

1870.

OUR LITTLE COMFORT.

CHAPTER I.

VERY few children ever passed Mr. Foster's tall brick house without thinking, "What a gloomy looking place! I would not live in it for the world." And so it was a dreary dwelling. The color had once been dark red, but now it was a dingy brown, excepting the spots where the paint had entirely worn off, and the door was almost black, with a great brass knob so high up that no child could ever reach that, nor the huge knocker above it. But very few persons ever went in or out of that desolate house but a middle-aged man and two servants, for Mrs. Foster had been confined to her bed for a whole year, and her husband was away all day. The blinds were all closed excepting a little one in the dining room, and the two in the chamber of the sick lady, and sometimes the whole house looked so quiet that passers by thought that every body in it certainly must have died.

But there was one bright, cheerful sound occasionally heard in Mrs. Foster's chamber, which she called the "singing of her nightingale." I am sure no other bird would have thought of raising its voice in such a dark place, for thick green curtains shut out almost all the light that came through the dingy blinds in the day time, and, at night, the only lamp was a little taper, and a screen hid that from the weak eyes of the sufferer. The great rough-looking nurse, Fanny, though she stepped very heavily, always spoke in a whisper, and Mr. Foster was so deaf that no one could hold any conversation with him, for he could hardly catch a single word, and when his poor wife wanted to make him understand anything, she had to write on his hand with one of her slender fingers, and that she might do so conveniently, he generally, when at home, seated himself in the big brown leather chair beside her bed.

But though Mrs. Foster called the lively sound to which we referred, the singing of her nightingale, it was the crowing of a little baby, a sweet dear little girl, about ten months old. Its mother was so sick that she could not always bear to have the child in her room, but sometimes Fanny brought it up from the dark cellar kitchen where she liked to stay so as to chat with the fat old cook, and then the little thing seemed like a ray of sunlight in that darkened chamber. Mrs. Foster had lost four children, and could hardly look at the one that was left without a fear that it might be taken from her, but she tried to smile when the bright little creature was seated on the bed by her side, and then Comfort would crow and laugh as merrily as a bird.

Perhaps you did not think that Comfort was the real name of a child, and it is not a very pretty one, but Mr. Foster, who doted on his baby, would not hear of her being named anything else.

She was fair as a lily, with eyes the color of a Forget-me-not, and soft, golden hair, which curled in funny little rings all over the top of her head. "Oh, if she would only say mama," thought Mrs. Foster, as she felt that little soft hand smoothing her own thin, pale cheek, while unintelligible, but very sweet, sounds poured from the rosy lips of her darling. Then the poor lady thought of the time when her lost Harry had first lisped that word, and how long it was before his sister Kate could master it, and she remembered how pleased the little boy had been with the very corals which were now looping up Comfort's sleeves, and how often he had worn the same white dress which she had on, and tears rolled out on her face and wet the soft hands that were still feeling it so gently. But Comfort knew nothing of sorrow, and seldom cried, only when she was a little uneasy or thought it was time that her milk bottle should appear, so she could not know anything of her mother's feelings, and therefore she kept on laughing and crowing, and putting her fingers almost into those wet, moist eyes, till the tears were all dried.

Now this little baby never dreamed that she was doing good to anybody by her cunning ways, but a young angel could hardly have done more to cheer the heart of her sick mother. For children are, from their birth, little missionaries sent to cheer and console those who are tired and sorrowful. God meant everybody in the world to be just as happy, and so they all would have been if no one had ever sinned, but now, older people are often full of care and sorrow, and therefore every child should remember that it is their part to do all in their power to gladden the hearts and lives of their parents.

Although Mr. Foster was so deaf, he was not a very old man, but he was odd, and many people did not know what to make of him.

He had always lived in Canada till about a year before Comfort was born, and then he became so deaf that he could not practise his profession, and so he left his native place and settled near Granville. There was no house to let in the neighborhood but the desolate looking one that we have described, and that had not been occupied for many years, for it was not on any public road and was two miles from the town. But Mrs. Foster had been so saddened by the recent death of her fourth child, that the idea of such a retired home was very welcome, and so the family moved into it, a few weeks after their arrival at Granville, and before they became acquainted with any of the inhabitants. Mrs. Foster never went outside of the door till Comfort was born, and after that, she was too ill to leave her bed, and her husband did not care about mak-

ing anything look comfortable, for since
he became so deaf, he had been an altered
man. Before that time, he was ambi-
tious, and everybody called him a very
talented lawyer, but of course, he could
no longer speak in court, as he was un-
able to hear any reply which might be
made to what he said. Some of his
friends wanted him to try and use an
ear-trumpet, but just from the fear of
looking ridiculous, he refused this assistance and determined that he would never
plead another case.

It is a strange idea for persons to be
angry because God takes away one of
those gifts which He bestows upon them,
but Mr. Foster felt as if he were really
injured, when he found that this infir-
mity was coming upon him, and grew
so cross and peevish that it made his
poor wife very unhappy. Even the books
of which he used to be so fond, did not

now seem to give him any pleasure, and
when he came home from the bank, where
he had a situation which kept him employed in writing, he would often go and
sit on the other side of the room, so that
Mrs. Foster could not write on his hand,
or find any way of talking to him. But
if while he was indulging himself in one
of these wicked, sulky fits, the baby was
brought into the chamber, he immediately looked like an entirely different
man. His big watch was drawn out to
be shaken before the eyes of the delighted little one, and he would toss her
so high in the air that her anxious
mother sometimes uttered a feeble cry
of alarm, which did not, however, reach
his deafened ear. He loved to put her
on the floor and let her try her skill in
creeping, and before she was eleven
months old Comfort could stand up by
a chair and play with a rattle-box, which

was the whole extent of the toys that she possessed.

A little while after Comfort was born, Mrs. Foster asked her husband if he would not send for a clergyman from Granville to come and christen the child, as she was afraid it would be very long before she should be able to go to church, but he replied that she would soon be better, and that there was no use in being in a hurry about the matter. He had been sponsor for his other children, although he had never professed to be a Christian man, but now he was in such a wicked, rebellious state of mind that he felt ashamed to assume such an office, and that was the reason why he kept putting off the baptism of the baby.

But when Comfort was three months old, she was taken very sick with the croup, and her mother and Fanny were almost sure that she would not get well, and then Mr. Foster was frightened, and thought God was going to take his child away to punish him for being so wicked. He went immediately to Granville, for the doctor and clergyman, and the latter not only baptized the child, but was its sponsor. There is no doubt that he would have been an excellent friend to Comfort, but he was taken ill in a few weeks and died, so that Mrs. Foster was the only one left to teach the child when she grew up what a solemn vow and promise had been made in her name.

And now, my young readers, you are expecting that our little friend will have a very gloomy life, but you are mistaken. Those are always the happiest who are the cause of joy to others, and Comfort Foster had a much fairer prospect of happiness than many a child who is surrounded by gay companions. She would soon learn that her sick

mother depended upon her for cheerful-
ness, and that by her little caresses she
could bring a smile to her father's stern
brow, so that she would feel herself of
use, and there are no children too young
to find that a pleasure. If you do not
believe it, go and try to make somebody
feel brighter and happier by a kind look
or word, carry a flower to the sick and
smooth their pillow, or give some mark
of affection and sympathy to the sorrowful, and when you see what pleasure
there is in even offering a glass of water
in a right spirit, you will understand
why no child is in danger of being
wretched except she is one who is wrapt
up in herself.

When Comfort was four years old,
she was one of the dearest little things
in the world. Her golden hair was no
longer in little rings on the top of her
head, but fell round her sweet face in

long bright curls, and her laugh was such a merry sound that the very birds seemed won by it to build their nests in the grim old poplars that rose above her home, where they did their best to make music as sweet.

It seemed as if the child knew how anxious her mother was that she should be old enough for a companion, for after she began to speak, her tongue was never weary of talking, and she said many things that were quite remarkable for such a little girl. Mrs. Foster's sad heart had been for a long time shut up in her own breast, but now she was so pleased to have some one to whom she could speak freely of her lost children, that she would spend hours in telling Comfort about her brothers and sisters, till the little girl felt as if she had known and loved them all. "And where are they now?" she asked eagerly, as she knelt by the bed, and looked lovingly into the pale, sweet face that had lain so long on that pillow.

"In a beautiful place, called Heaven," was the reply, "where I hope that my little Comfort will one day see them all. You know that I told you that besides your father, whom you see every day, you had another one, to whom you speak every night before you go to sleep. Although He can hear all that you say, and knows each thought that passes through your mind, the place where He lives is not in this world, but is called Heaven. It is so beautiful that any one, after seeing it, would never want to come away, so He takes no one there till He is ready to have them go and live with Him forever. Our little Katy seemed very happy when she heard that God was willing that she should go to that delightful home, and smiled so sweetly when she went away, that I thought that she looked like the angels who have always lived where there is no weeping or sorrow."

"Does nobody cry in Heaven?" asked Comfort, eagerly.

"No, my child," said her mother, "for there is no pain nor sickness there, nei ther does any one ever do wrong, which, you know, is what makes us more un- happy here than anything else."

"Mother!" said little Comfort, in a most earnest tone, "I am going to ask God to let me come and live with Him and my little brothers and sisters in Heaven. Don't you think He will be kind enough to take me if I say, 'Please, for Christ's sake?' You know that you said He would give me what I wanted, if it was right, and I am sure that He won't be angry because I want to come and see His pretty home."

2*

Mrs. Foster was somewhat startled at these words, and an expression of pain came over her face, while her eyes filled with tears.

"Don't talk so, my darling," she said quickly, "you frighten me."

"Frighten you, mama," repeated Comfort, in astonishment. "Didn't you say that my brothers and sisters were happy? What makes you frightened when I say I should like to be with them?"

"Because I could not spare our little Comfort," replied Mrs. Foster, sadly, as she laid her thin hand on the soft curls of her child. "Are you not willing to stay here with me? God does not think that I have lived in this world long enough yet, and you would not wish to leave your poor, sick mother, all alone."

"Oh no!" said the child, affectionately, "I will stay with you as long as you want me ; but don't you hope that before a great while we may both go and live in that beautiful place together ?"

Mrs. Foster did not reply, but after this conversation, Comfort always felt as if she were left in this world, instead of going to live with her brothers and sisters, because God knew that her sick mother needed a companion, and it was, therefore, her first thought to try and cheer her loneliness.

Mrs. Foster had taught her child what it was to pray, before she could speak plain, and had tried so hard to make her feel that God was her kindest friend, that sometimes Comfort's prayers sounded strangely familiar. She would tell all her little joys and sorrows as if she were talking to her mother, and the night after she had been told where her brothers and sisters were, Mrs. Foster saw her kneel down at the foot of her bed, and heard her say, "Oh, my dear, good heavenly Father, I wish I could come and live with you, but mama says she wants me to stay here." Won't you tell me how to be a good little girl, for mama says bad children won't ever come to your pretty home, and I do so want to see it, and I hope by and by you'll let us both come, and then what a happy time we shall have."

Another evening, the little girl was so delighted with a box of letters that her father had bought for her at Granville, that she dropped right down on her knees in the middle of the floor to thank Him from whom, she had been told, all her pleasures proceeded. Sometimes her way of speaking did not seem to her mother quite proper, but she did not know how to make her understand what a great Being God was, without her becoming afraid of Him, and she hoped that His pure eye would accept the simple faith of the child and **pardon** anything that might be amiss in her manner or words.

There was a large Bible and a Prayer Book always lying upon the stand beside Mrs. Foster's bed, and Fanny, who could hardly read correctly, used to spell out a few verses to her mistress every morning, but it was not always easy to find out what they were about, for the kind-hearted nurse was but a poor scholar. After this reading was over, Mrs. Foster would sometimes tell Fanny to lay the Bible on the bed, by her, and then **Comfort** would clamber up beside it, and her mother would show the little girl all the pictures, and tell her short stories about Joseph and Samuel, and about the child-hood of our Saviour.

One evening, just at sundown, the sick lady had fallen asleep when **Mr.** Foster came home from the bank, and, taking his little girl on his knee, asked if she could say all her letters. Comfort was delighted to answer "Yes," and, jumping down, she ran and got the little ivory box from the lowest drawer in her mother's bureau, where it was always kept. Having emptied the letters all on the carpet, she drew back the curtain, so as to let in a little more light, and then made signs to her father to call for any one that he chose. Mr. Foster watched her motions with fond affection, and beginning at the end of the alphabet, called out the letters backward, and they were all brought to him without a single mistake.

When Comfort had thus convinced her father that she knew all the contents of her beloved ivory box, she was seized with a desire to look over the pictures in the Bible and hear some of her favorite stories, but with all her signs and gestures she could not make her father

understand what she wanted. The heavy
book was lying at the foot of her mother's
bed, but she could not lift it down and
did not like to ask her father to get it,
for she knew he was tired and did not
want to move. For some time she sat
eyeing it very wistfully, and then she
jumped up and down, clapping her hands
as if she had just had a very bright
thought. Her father did not know what
she was about, till he saw her take a long
string off from a little footstool, which
she called her "carriage," and fasten it
around the Bible. Then she slowly
drew the book off the bed, standing close
by it, so that it might not make a noise
coming down to the ground, and when
this was done she dragged it round to
her father's chair, where she stood pointing at it with such a winning smile, that
he could not resist her wishes. He took
the book up on one knee and the little

girl on the other, and after he had showed her all the pictures, told her the stories which he had liked best when a child, and which he had not thought of for many years.

Comfort, who now slept in a little crib in the same room with her father and mother, had often wondered why Mr. Foster never said any prayers mornings or evenings, but his deafness rendered it impossible for her to make him understand all that she wished to tell him, so that he was not aware of the idea that was working in her little brain. But now she thought she had a good chance to ask if men ought not to pray as well as children, so when they came to the picture of little Samuel, she pointed first to him and then herself, as much as to say, "He prayed and I pray," and then making him turn back to a picture of Jacob kneeling at Bethel, she looked at him, and her face said, as plain as words, "Father, ought you not to do the same?"

Mr. Foster did not answer this earnest appeal, but that night, as little Comfort lay in her crib, she saw her father kneeling at the foot of the bed, and she went to sleep with a happy heart.

CHAPTER II.

When his little daughter was six years old, Mr. Foster proposed, one Sabbath morning, that she should go with him to Granville, to church.   Mrs. Foster's eyes filled with tears of pleasure at these words, for her husband had never been to church, himself, since he had become so deaf, because he said there was no use in going when he could not hear a word that the clergyman read or preached. "But you could keep up with the service," his wife would reply, "and find the lessons, and worship God with the congregation."

" I can read the Prayer Book at home," was his answer; but this he never did, like most people who make the same excuse for not going to church. Now that he really felt a desire to do right he could not be contented without a more public acknowledgment of his dependence upon his Maker.

Mrs. Foster rang the bell at the head of her bed, for Fanny, and then she began to think what Comfort would wear to church, for the little girl had no clothes, only such as had belonged to her sisters, or were made out of her mother's, and these were very queer and old-fashioned. At first, the fond mother wished that her darling had some less peculiar look-ing garments, but she remembered that we should always dress according to the society into which we are going, and that the best preparation for entering the presence of our Maker is a clean heart and a right spirit.

When Fanny answered the bell, Com-fort came with her, and the child was almost wild with joy at hearing that she was to go to church with her father. She had never been to Granville in her life, and as she took all her walks in the retired roads around the house, she rarely saw anybody but her own family.

But it was not only the idea of going to the village which excited the little girl, but the thought of entering a church, which her mother always mentioned as the place of all others that she most wished to visit. It is true that Comfort had no very clear idea of what a church was, and having confused it with the many descriptions that she had heard of Heaven, one of her first questions was, "Shall I see my brothers and sisters, and will Jesus Christ be there, looking like the little boy in the Temple, with the Doctors?"

Mrs. Foster smiled at the childish thought, and tried to teach Comfort how

God could be present and not be seen, as He was everywhere, and how the minister was sent by the Lord Jesus to speak the words taken out of Holy Scripture, and therefore ought to be listened to very attentively and humbly.

Comfort looked very intelligent during this explanation, but I do not think that she yet understood exactly what kind of a place she was going to, only she felt reverence for the man who was to be so honored as to tell the people what was the will of the Great Being who made them all.

While this conversation had been going on, Fanny had taken the little girl's clothes out of a trunk in the corner of the room, and hung them over the back of the old chintz lounge, and now she called to her to come and put on a pair of blue gaiter boots which had once been her sister Kate's, and

which she had never seen before. They
were a little too large, and so was the
grey silk pelisse which had been made
out of an old frock of her mother's, but
Comfort seemed to think that they were
very nice, and that the round white hat,
with a pearl buckle at the side, was exceedingly beautiful. Still, she did not
pay much attention to either of these
things after her first exclamation of admiration, for she had never seen any
one who thought much of dress, and
her mother always told her that her
body, and its covering, must be laid
aside when she went to the beautiful
world where her sisters lived, and, as
she was constantly looking forward with
pleasure to that time, of course she did
not overvalue what would then be of
no consequence. She chattered away
while Fanny buttoned up her red dress
and put on the grey pelisse, and did

not even stop while her ringlets were being curled, though Fanny sometimes pulled them very hard as she was brushing them around her great red fingers.

Mrs. Foster could not help thinking, when her little girl was dressed, that she was a pretty creature in spite of her old-fashioned clothes, and she wondered how anybody could imagine it of any consequence what a child wore, when a sweet expression and tidy habits could always make it attractive.

"Now, Fanny," she said, "go to the big trunk in the next room and take out my purple Prayer Book. Comfort shall carry that, to-day, to church, and when she reads the prayer for all sick persons, she will think, I know, of her poor mother."

Comfort was not too much occupied with her curiosity as to the treasure with which she was to be intrusted, to

pay attention to what her mother said,
for she walked very soberly to the bedside and said, as she put up her pretty
little mouth for a kiss, "I will get all
the people, mother, to ask God to make
you well, for you know that you said
if two or three asked for a thing together
He liked to do it. I shall be one, and
father makes two, and if we can get somebody else to help us there will be three,
and then, perhaps, God will cure you,
and you can go to church yourself."

Mrs. Foster smiled at the simple faith
of the child, and handed her the pretty
purple Prayer Book after she had put
the red marks in the places where they
would be needed.

Comfort had learned to read almost
by herself after her father had taught
her to say the ivory letters, and as she
had only two little books, which did not
long satisfy her curiosity, she had spent

many hours in spelling out the words at the bottom of the pictures in the big Bible, till she seldom found one that puzzled her. For the last three months she had read a Psalm every day, aloud, to her mother, and it was pleasant to see her soft curls bending over the old Bible, while her little plump finger kept the place, and sometimes she would look up with such a thoughtful air, and make some remark that showed that she was interested in what she read.

Mr. Foster came into the room soon after Comfort was dressed, and, taking her up in his arms, called her "a little darling," and hoped that she would be very quiet and good, and remember what the minister said, so as to come home and tell her mother. Then he led her down the dark, narrow stairs, and through the big black door, out into the pleasant air of a fine spring morning.

The birds were singing merrily, and Comfort said she guessed they were glad that she was going to church, and one or two wagons passed them, loaded with people all in their Sunday clothes. The little girl skipped and jumped along, gathering violets and forget-me-nots from the borders of the meadows through which they passed, till one little hand was quite full, and she let go her father's so as to carry her Prayer Book in the other. She did not feel at all tired when they had walked almost a mile, but Mr. Foster insisted on carrying her, and did not put her down till they were near the town.

Though Comfort had never seen but very few houses, those which they passed did not seem to excite her admiration so much as the gardens adjoining them, and when they came to one which had a large conservatory, through which a lemon-tree was visible, covered with its yellow fruit, the little girl was almost wild with delight. "Oh, father! how many pretty things God can make," she exclaimed; "mustn't He be good?" And though Mr. Foster could not hear what she said, he was struck with her expression of earnest thankfulness.

"There, there! that's the church, isn't it, father? I mean the one that's pointing at heaven," said Comfort, with great animation as they came near a large stone building, with a tall spire, surmounted by a cross.

Several persons, who were going thither were attracted by her expressions of delight, and thought what an odd-looking man that was, and wondered where such a queer, pretty little girl came from, and how it happened that she had never seen the church before. They did not know about the sick mother who had never left her bed since Comfort's birth, or how her deaf father had, when first afflicted, gone farther off from God, instead of drawing nigh to Him.

Mr. Foster did not feel as happy as his child, for men who have neglected religion must always go through a great deal more in coming back to their heavenly Father, for you know the Prodigal Son suffered much before he returned to his dear parent.

But though Comfort was so full of joy, the moment that she stepped inside of the church door, her whole manner changed. She thought that the voluntary on the organ was the song of the angels, and fancied that some of the low, sweet notes were the voices of her brothers and sisters. Her blue eyes were full of tears at this idea, and yet there was a happy smile on her lips, and the pure young blood seemed ready to start from her transparent cheeks. She hardly needed to notice that everybody else knelt down on entering the church, for her heart was so full of thankfulness to be in such a holy place, that it seemed the most natural thing in the world. Her little, simple prayer was not unlike the expression of the Psalmist, "I was glad when they said unto me, let us go into the house of the Lord," for her words were, "Dear Saviour, I am so glad to be here. Tell me what to do and what to say, and when I go home, don't let me forget how kind you have been."

Perhaps these simple prayers may seem strange, but Comfort had had no instruction only from her sick mother, who was often too ill to explain to her all that she wished, but she had read much in the Bible and Prayer Book, and had formed an idea that God was the kindest, dearest friend that she had, and I am

4

sure that this was right. Soon after Mr.
Foster and his little girl were seated in
church, a lady and two children came
into the pew to which he had been shown
by the sexton, and took possession of the
upper end, as Comfort had seated herself
close to her father. The lady was very
handsomely dressed, and so were both
her daughters, but the faces of the children were by no means as agreeable as
that of their mother. Neither of the
little girls bowed their heads, or showed
any mark of reverence on entering the
church; but, on the contrary, they commenced whispering so loudly, that Comfort could not help hearing what they said.

"I should think," remarked the elder,
"that she imagined that she was in her
own pew, by the quiet way in which
she has taken possession of ours."

This speech was quite lost on the
simple-hearted person to whom it re-

ferred, for "Comfort had heard that she was going to the house of God, and she thought that she had as much claim to any part of it as the rest of His children.

"Did you ever see such a queer little thing?" continued the first speaker, who was a tall girl of about ten years old. "Is she a woman or a child? she is dressed like one and looks like the other. That old silk pelisse must have come out of the ark, and I am sure Noah's youngest grandchild used to wear that hat."

The only effect that these rude words had upon Comfort, was to excite her un-mingled astonishment and pity. "Those girls have never heard that God made them," she thought, "or they would not dare to act so in His house."

With the full belief that her com-panions were some of the unfortunate heathen of whom her mother had told her, the earnest little girl leaned forward, kindly, so as to speak to the elder of the two children, without being overheard, and said, "This house belongs to a very great Being, called God, who made us all, and He is angry when His children do not love Him, and He punishes those that displease Him. These books here," she added, pointing to the Prayer Books which lay in the seat, "will tell you about Him, and how he likes to have us act in His house. Here is what He says Himself." And opening her own book, she showed the text at the commencement of the Morning Service, "The Lord is in His holy temple; let all the earth keep silence before Him.

At these remarks, the two children both laughed aloud, in spite of the reproving looks of their mother, who could not imagine what the stranger had said to excite their mirth. She was still more puzzled to account for it, when, on turning to look at Comfort, she saw that the little girl's face was not only serious, but expressed the greatest sorrow and alarm.

Comfort had read in the Bible what dreadful punishments God sometimes inflicted on those who displeased Him, and as she thought how wicked these children must appear in His eyes, she almost expected to see lightning coming down from heaven to destroy them. She did not know that though God is still angry with sin, He sometimes puts off its punishment, and that each word and act of those irreverent children was written down in a book which would be read at the day of judgment.

The voice of the minister, as he commenced the Morning Service, quieted Comfort's mind, and, such is the force of example, that her young companions opened their Prayer Books and listened to the Exhortation. They did not join, however, in the following Confession of Sin, in which Comfort spoke very distinctly, for, though we have not told of the naughty things that she did, she had been guilty of many acts and words that needed repentance. Mr. Foster's voice, too, sounded very solemn, for he had not only the unconfessed sins of a day, or week, to lament, but those of the long years which had passed since he last knelt in the house of prayer.

The first Morning Lesson was one of those chapters in Numbers, that gives an account of the manner in which the children of Israel angered God in the wilderness, and Comfort turned round to see if the little girls beside her were not frightened to learn how dangerous it was to provoke such a powerful Being, but they seemed entirely occupied with their own clothes, taking their kid gloves off, and looking to see how much difference there was in the patterns of their embroidered handkerchiefs.

"I wonder if they are going to live in this world for ever," thought Comfort, "for mama said, that when we went out of it, we could carry nothing with us, and I am sure they would not be so fond of their clothes, if they must take them off when they are called away. But, perhaps, they are going to the bad world! maybe people can carry what they like there, for the very ones that set their hearts on what they have here, the Bible says, will have to live there. Oh, how dreadful it is to think such dear little girls may go to such an awful place!" And then the tears filled those sweet blue eyes, and a sob burst from her troubled heart.

Mr. Foster saw that his little girl was crying, and asked her if anything was the matter, but she only shook her head, while her heart heaved with emotion. It was a relief to her when everybody knelt down again, and she could hide her face in the cushion and cry to her heart's content. She joined earnestly in the Lenten Collect, particularly praying that God would give her young companions new and contrite hearts. Some little girls may not know what the word "contrite" means, but Comfort was never satisfied to say a prayer till she understood every word of it, and, before Lent began, her mother had read over the Collect for Ash-Wednesday, and explained it very fully.

The hymn which was sung by the congregation after the service was read, was the pretty one which begins,

> "Oh, in the morn of life
>   When youth with vital ardor glows,
> And shines in all the fairest charms
>   That beauty can disclose."

Comfort again thought, when the organ played, that the angels were joining in the singing.

The moment that the clergyman went up into the pulpit, the little girl prepared to give her whole attention to what he said, for she remembered what her mother had told her, and felt as if she were going to hear a message from her heavenly Father. There were many words in the sermon which she did not understand, but the text was, " Remember thy Creator in the days of thy youth," and that was so pretty that she never tired of hearing it repeated.

Mr. Foster, during the sermon, was thinking very deeply, and perhaps his own meditations on that day did him as much good as any discourse could have done. It is certain that his face was more cheerful than Comfort had ever seen it, when, at the close of the services, he took his little girl by the hand to lead her out of church. Before they left the pew, the lady who was sitting at the head of it asked Comfort what was her name, and where she lived. "I wish you would come and see my little girls," she added, "for I am sure that a child who behaves so well in church would be a nice companion for them."

Comfort wondered why any one should praise her for doing only what was right, and what she should be afraid not to do, but she answered very simply and sweetly, saying, that she had a sick mother who could not spare her, but who would like, she was sure, to have any little girls come and see her, "only," she added, very earnestly, "perhaps mama would not wish to have me much with any children who do not love the great God well enough to obey Him.

She is never angry with me only when
I do wrong, and I don't think she would
like it if your little girls said anything
naughty before her."

"You are a queer little thing," said
the lady, who was puzzled by the manner and conversation of the child. ' Ask
your father if you may not come and
see me. I live at the large stone house
just below the church."

"He could not hear me," replied Comfort, "and indeed, do you think it is
right for us to be talking in church?
Had we not better wait till we get out
doors before we say any more?"

"Certainly," replied the lady, hastily,
"only always sit here when you come
to church."

Comfort bowed in acknowledgment of
this offer, but, without opening her lips
again, took her father's hand and walked
quietly out of church. She did not speak

till they were quite in the country, and
then she looked up in her father's face
and said, "Was it not nice to be there!"
He understood her words from the motion
of her lips, and, stooping down, kissed
her tenderly, and asked if she would not
like to be carried a little way.

Comfort assured him that she was not
in the least tired, and so they walked on
in silence, but the child now and then
lifted her blue eyes to the deeper blue
sky, and tried to think how Heaven
would look, and wondered how long it
would be before she should learn to sing
the song of angels. She stopped, however, to gather some fresh flowers for
her mother, having left those in the pew
which she had taken to church, and she
was delighted to find some anemones and
sweet-scented white violets that she particularly loved. The tall, dingy house
looked really pleasant to her as they

came near it, for she knew it contained
her dear mother, and a happy heart
makes everything appear bright. She
could hardly wait for her father to open
the door, and then she bounded up the
long dark stairs, and running into her
mother's chamber, exclaimed,

"Dear, dear mama, you will certainly
be well, for everybody prayed for all
sick persons."

5

CHAPTER III.

It was wonderful to see how every
room in Mr. Foster's house changed after
Comfort was able to run about and play
in them all. The little back dining room
had before been a dreary looking place,
but now it began to have quite an inhabited air. While Mr. Foster ate his
meals there, all by himself, the table was
never moved out from the wall, and one
solitary plate was set at the end of it,
with the other dishes crowded around,
in the greatest confusion. Now, the table
stood in the middle of the floor, regularly
laid for two people, with a pretty silver
cup, and a knife and fork of the same
metal, at the plate before it. These were
a present to Comfort from an aunt who

lived in England, and she thought a great deal of them, not because they were expensive, for I do not believe that she had the slightest idea what was the price of anything, but because they could not be broken, and she could therefore keep them always to remember a relative of whom she had heard her mother speak with so much affection.

Mr. Foster did not come home to dinner, so the little girl ate that meal with her mother, but at tea and breakfast she would often try and lift the small old fashioned tea-pot, so as to fill her father's cup; and before she was strong enough for this, she insisted on putting the milk and sugar, at least, into it, with her own plump, little, white hands.

The next evening after Comfort went to Granville church, as her mother was asleep, she came down into the dining-room to wait for Mr. Foster's return from

the bank, and was perched up in her
little chair, looking as bright as a star,
when he opened the door. She sprang
down to welcome him, and tugged away
at the sleeve of his overcoat, which was
damp with a spring shower, and then
took her seat at the table again as if
she were quite a woman. All at once
the little girl spied the funniest looking
thing in the chair beside her father, and
forgetting that she was going to pour
out his tea, she jumped down again from
her seat, and taking up the queer con-
trivance of green tin, began to make
all manner of signs to learn what it
might be. She put it over a cup to ask
if it were a funnel, and then turned it
upside down and stuck her finger in the
end to inquire if it was a candlestick,
while Mr. Foster sat smiling at her curiosity.

At length, with rather a sad expression, he took a long tube from his pocket, and attaching it to the green funnel-shaped mouth-piece, put one end in his ear.

The idea now struck Comfort what the queer thing was, but she thought that her father would look very funny with such a thing always in his ear, and she pushed it away with her hand, saying quickly,—

"Oh, don't, father, it makes you look so."

Although Mr. Foster did not know what the child said, her motion was very expressive, and his face grew more grave, but in a moment he conquered the unpleasant feeling, and said cheerfully,—

"I wanted to hear the sound of my little daughter's voice. Speak through this, my dear, and see if I can hear what you say."

Comfort sprang to his knee, and putting the trumpet to her mouth, said very distinctly,—

"My dear father, how happy I should be if I could only talk to you as much as I wished."

The words were hardly spoken before he clasped her in his arms, and kissing her tenderly, exclaimed,—

"What a blessed sound! I heard you perfectly, my child, and your voice was sweeter to me than any music. How could I have so long allowed my pride to deprive me of this unspeakable pleasure!"

Comfort wondered what he meant by these last words, but she was too much delighted to think of them long.

"Oh, let us go right up stairs to mama," she exclaimed, "won't she be glad to speak to you once more? She was asleep when I came down, but it will make her so happy to talk to you that she won't mind being waked up, I'm sure."

Mr. Foster, however, thought that it was best not to disturb his wife till after supper, but Comfort gave up all idea of making tea, and got Fanny to bring her chair round close to her father's, and never let go the ear-trumpet till he insisted on her taking time to eat. Then she swallowed a few mouthfuls in silence, but suddenly some thought struck her, which she could not keep to herself, and she again seized the tube and said, very earnestly,—

"Father, I read in the Bible that when they were building the tabernacle, God made two men very wise, on purpose that they might do some very cunning work. Did he make another man wise, too, so that you might have this ear-trumpet and talk to mama?"

"Perhaps so," replied Mr. Foster, who

wondered how such an idea came into the child's head, and how she happened to notice the verses about Bezaleel and Aholiab in the 35th chapter of Exodus.

"Father," said Comfort, again putting down her knife and fork to take hold of the ear-trumpet, "don't it seem just like our Saviour to make you hear again? You know He was always curing the deaf; and though I never read of anybody that He gave such a thing to, yet it shows the same love to teach somebody how to make it. Doesn't it?"

"Yes, my child, God has been very kind to me!" replied Mr. Foster; and it was almost the first time that Comfort had ever heard him speak of the Being who was so much in her own thoughts.

"May I tell mama, now?" she asked, as she saw that her father had finished his supper.

"If she is awake," was the answer; and before Mr. Foster could reach his wife's chamber, Comfort was seated on her bed, telling her that God had taught somebody how to make her father a new ear, so that he could hear all that everybody said. Mrs. Foster did not understand exactly what the delighted child meant; but when she saw the ear-trumpet her heart overflowed with thankfulness that her husband had, at last, consented to use such an instrument. He came to her bedside, and kissed her with uncommon tenderness; and then seating himself in the great leather chair, enjoyed the first conversation with his wife which he had had for eight years.

In the mean time, Comfort sat on his knee, with her head on his bosom, never interrupting him, but showing by her animated face how deeply she sympathized in her mother's joy. When it came time for her to go to bed, she could not sleep; for, instead of the silence that there always was in the room, when her own tongue was still, she could hear her father's voice, and the gentle tones of his delicate wife.

As the little girl grew drowsy, her thoughts became somewhat composed; but the last one before she dropped asleep was of the goodness and greatness of her Heavenly Father.

At daylight, the next morning, Mr. Foster was awakened by hearing a sweet voice saying the hymn,

"When streaming from the eastern skies,
The morning light salutes mine eyes,
O Sun of Righteousness divine,
On me with beams of mercy shine;
Chase the dark clouds of sin away,
And turn my darkness into day."

Was he dreaming, or had he recovered his hearing during the night?

He had forgotten all about the ear-trumpet, but on opening his eyes, saw little Comfort in her nightgown, with her golden hair floating round her smiling face, holding the tube in one hand, while the other kept it firm in his ear. With the rosy light of dawn, brightening her fair skin, she might well have been mistaken for some good angel, who had been watching over his sleep; and with her smile there mingled a sweet earnestness, befitting the words that she had just repeated.

"Will you hear me read, father?" asked the little girl. "I thought you would like to wake up early, this morning, because you had so much to thank our Heavenly Father for; and that perhaps I might help you by reading a psalm while you were shaving. Would you like that, dear papa?"

"Could you, my dear, keep your eyes on your book and at the same time speak through my trumpet? and won't it be a hard task for me to hold my head still while I am shaving and dressing? But I will get up now, and there will be time, after I have done, for you to repeat to me some nice verses that you have learned, and that will do as well as if you read them."

Comfort looked a little disappointed, but she was consoled by her father letting her go herself for his shaving cup, which was in the next room, and then she lay down again, and thought over all the Psalms and texts she knew, so as to choose some to recite to him when he was ready to hear her.

When Mr. Foster was dressed, he rang the bell for Fanny, and then he told Comfort that she could get up, and that as soon as she was ready for breakfast she must come down into the dining-room. When her father had gone, Comfort jumped out of her crib and popped into the bath, which Fanny had filled, just like a little duck, for she loved dearly to be in the water. But she came out the moment that her nurse said it was time, and put on the clothes that were laid on the chair as quickly as possible, without making any objection to one of them.

My little readers may think that Comfort had not any taste, but they are mistaken, for she very much preferred some colors to others, and had a particular fancy for wearing white dresses. But she knew that her blue mousseline de laine was much better for April, and so she said it looked like the sky, and though the frock had been worn all winter, it had not a single stain. The little girl was very particular about keeping her clothes nice, and if the least speck got on one of her favorite white dresses, she would look at it with the most mournful

6

expression, for she had been told that
cleanliness was an emblem of holiness,
and thought that God liked purity of
body as well as purity of soul. For the
same reason, she never wanted to say her
prayers till she had taken her bath. "I
know He can see me always," she would
say to her nurse, "but I like to be clean
when I speak to Him." Her mother
could not think how her little daughter
got this idea, but Comfort showed her the
place in the Bible where God told the
Israelites to wash their clothes before they
came near to Mount Sinai, and the law
that He made, that the priests should
always wear perfectly pure garments
when they came to perform the service
of the sanctuary.

It was her own childish notion, but
she was very right in thinking that out-
ward cleanliness was a sign of inward
purity, for you know that in baptism,

the washing of water is the emblem of the cleansing of our souls through the blood of Christ.

When Comfort was dressed, she knelt down and thanked God for His care of her during the past night, and for all His blessings, and mentioned particularly the new ear-trumpet through which she could speak to her father, and she asked her heavenly Friend never to let her say anything to her father which would give him any pain, and to make her more useful, every day, to both her dear parents.

When she rose from her knees, the little girl stole on tiptoe to the bed, and gently kissed her mother, who was fast asleep, and then she went down stairs with Fanny, skipping along like a little fawn, and singing as she went.

On entering the dining-room, Comfort found her father reading, and as soon as

he saw her he told Fanny to ask the cook
if she could come in for a few minutes,
for he was going to have family prayers.
Comfort had never heard of such a thing
before, but she sat down on her father's
knee, very quietly, and he found the
lesson for the day in the small Bible that
he had taken out of the book-case, and
then the service in the Prayer Book for.
family worship.

The little girl could not help thinking
of the minister at church when she heard
her father's voice, sounding so solemn,
as he read the chapter for that morning,
and she felt as if he were going to be
a clergyman to his own family. Just as
they were kneeling down she wanted to
ask him to pray for her mother, but she
was afraid it would not be right to do
so, and therefore she kept the thought
to herself, but her heart bounded with
joy when she heard her dear parent com-

mended to the care of God in a tone of deep tenderness, and when she tried to say Amen, a sob of joy burst from her full heart.

Comfort thought she had never loved her father so well as that morning, when, after the servants left the room, she was again seated on his knee. When he asked her to repeat a Psalm to him, all those that she had been thinking about went out of her mind, and the words burst from her lips, "Bless the Lord, O my soul, and all that is within me bless His holy name." When she· finished repeating this Psalm, her father made no remark, only he pressed her close to his bosom, saying, "My little Comfort!" in a tone of fond affection.

6*

CHAPTER IV.

MRS. FOSTER was so much of an invalid, that she did not generally wake
till after her husband had gone to the
bank, and lately, Comfort had walked
a little way with her father, though she
never went out of sight of the house, and
Fanny always followed her to bring her
home.   When she came back into the
yard, the little girl always visited a bird's
nest which was just built in a low quince
tree near the front door, and then she fed
her chickens, who each of them had a
name that she had given them, on account of some peculiarity in their appearance.   One, with a crest, was Toppy, and
his slender mate was Ladybird, and a
little sickly thing was " Pet," and a fat

old hen, "Mrs. Waddle." The tortoise-
shell cat, who was another of Comfort's
darlings, was too well brought up ever
to dream of troubling the chickens, but
it was very amusing to hear the way in
which she talked to her upon the subject.

But though the little girl was very
fond of all these dumb pets, she some
times felt as Adam did, when first placed
in the garden of Eden; that is, as if there
were no mate for herself among the
animals round her. She tried to imagine
that her little sisters might be looking
down at her, from their happy home;
and at night, when the stars shone, was
almost sure that they were the eyes of
angels: but still she longed for some
companion of her own age. She never
mentioned this wish, however, to her
mother; for she knew that the poor lady
was very sad when anything was said
that recalled the loss of her other chil

dren; so she contented herself with telling Fanny that she wished she had a little sister, or that her big doll could talk and play.

Poor Miss Dolly was obliged to be a variety of little people, with whom Comfort held long conversations—carrying on of course both parts of them herself. On the Tuesday morning, of which we have spoken, Comfort put her up in her own high chair, at the table in the dining-room; and then she seated herself in the one opposite, and imagined that she was Joseph, and Miss Dolly was Benjamin; and they were having a private meeting after they had discovered that they were brothers. "My dear Benjamin," said the imaginary Joseph, " were you very lively after I went away? and didn't you cry dreadfully when you found that I was never coming back?"

"Oh, yes!" said the same sweet little

voice, now pretending to be that of Benjamin. "I could not get to sleep at all, for thinking about it. I used to go and get in father's bed every night, and sometimes we lay and talked about you till morning. I tried to act as you did, so as to please father; but I could never be half as good. You never knew about the way that our brothers did to make us think you were dead. They took that pretty coat of yours and dipped it in blood, and showed it to father! and I thought he would have died when he saw it; and I am sure I was nearly frightened to death. He always kept that coat in his room; and I have often seen him crying over it as if his heart was breaking—I am sure, though, that Reuben felt almost as bad; for he never heard your name without looking very miserable."

"Were they kind to you—I mean your brothers?" asked the little Joseph.

"Oh, yes, they always treated me well, and though I knew they were so cruel to you, I can't help loving them, and I am so glad that you did not punish them."

The conversation was here interrupted by the entrance of Fanny, who came to say that Mrs. Foster was awake, and wanted to see her little girl. Benjamin immediately became Miss Dolly again, and was dragged up stairs by one arm, her old wooden head going bump, bump all the way.

Comfort had much to tell her mother, for she had not had an opportunity to say anything since the evening before, and everything she said was listened to as attentively as if it were the most important in the world. Two hours went by very quickly, and the tall old clock in the corner of the kitchen had just struck twelve, when Fanny came bustling into Mrs. Foster's room in a state of great excitement, and holding in her hand a visiting card.

"Oh dear," she said, "there's the most beautiful dressed lady come in a splendid carriage, and wants to see Mrs. Foster, and told me to give her this ticket, and fetch her back word whether she could come up."

"Where is she?" said Mrs. Foster, after looking at the card, on which was engraved the name of "Mrs. Henry Davis," and a line written below, to say that that lady would like to make the acquaintance of Mrs. Foster, if she were not too ill to see a stranger.

"Oh, in the parlor, ma'am, and it is as dark as Egypt and as damp as a dungeon, and I warrant her fine things will get well dusted, for the room hasn't been opened this six years."

Mrs. Foster thought a moment, and was on the point of declining to see the stranger, when the possibility glanced through her mind, that the time would come when her little daughter would stand in need of friends such as she hoped this lady might prove.

"Comfort, my dear," she said, "go down stairs very carefully, and be sure and not fall, and say to Mrs. Davis, that I shall be happy to see her in a few minutes. I will send Fanny for her when I am ready, and you must stay and talk to her till she comes."

Comfort never thought of not doing exactly as she was told, and though she had seen very few strangers, she did not feel the least awkwardness in now going into the room with her mother's message. When, however, she reached the parlor, it was so dark that she could not see any one, so she stopped at the door, and called out,—

"Mrs. Davis, are you in this disagreeable place. Won't you tell me where you are?"

"Here, my child," said a pleasant voice, and a lady rose from a chair near the door, and stepped into the hall. "We are old acquaintances, I think, and I have come partly to see you."

Comfort returned the kind kiss with which these words were accompanied, and recognized the visitor as the lady whom she had seen at church.

"Mama says that she would like to see you in a few moments," said the little girl, "but do not stay in that room, for I heard Fanny say that it was damp there, and you might take cold, and then you would be sick, like poor mama, and how sorry your little girls would feel."

"Will you show me your mother's room, then?" said Mrs. Davis. "Is that what you were to do?"

"No, ma'am; she will send Fanny for

7

us when she is ready to see you," replied Comfort, but she was puzzled what to do in the mean time with the lady, for the hall was a dreary place to stay in, and the cook was washing up the oil-cloth on the dining-room floor. " Shall I bring you a chair out of the parlor to sit here, or will you take a little walk and see the bird's nest in the quince tree, and Toppy, and Ladybird, and Pet, and Mrs. Waddle?" she asked, with the natural politeness of a kind heart.

" I will take a walk with pleasure," said Mrs. Davis.

" Then please open the door, for I can't reach the knob. Could your little girl?"

" Yes, I think Mary is tall enough," replied Mrs. Davis, as she opened the door, and, holding the hand of her companion, stepped out into the yard. She had only time enough to admire the one little speckled egg which had just been laid in the bird's nest, when Fanny came in search of the visitor, and was much surprised to find where Comfort had taken her. " Please excuse Miss Comfort," she said, "she thinks everybody likes birds' nests as well as herself."

" I have nothing to excuse," said Mrs. Davis, kindly; "she was doing the best she could to amuse me, and she is a dear little girl."

Comfort had been so much occupied in showing her treasure that she did not see the carriage at the gate, but in turning to come into the house it met her eye, and she exclaimed with delight, " Oh, what pretty horses, and what a nice carriage. You can go everywhere in the world, can't you, Mrs. Davis? Did you ever see Jerusalem?"

The lady smiled at the question, for she saw that Comfort thought that she could ride in a carriage to the place of

which she spoke, but she had time only
to say, "No, my darling, I never saw
Jerusalem," before she was shown into
Mrs. Foster's room.

We have not told our readers how
Mrs. Foster looked, but she was such
a nice lady that they must have been
sure that her appearance was very pleasant and attractive. She was sitting up
in bed, now, supported by pillows, with
a clean cap with a nicely plaited ruffle,
and she had on a dark dressing-gown
which Comfort had never seen before.

"You must forgive me for intruding
upon you," said Mrs. Davis, "but I saw
your little girl on Sunday, and have been
very anxious that my children should
make her acquaintance."

"I am indebted, then, to you," said
Mrs. Foster, "for the invitation to your
seat in church, of which Comfort told me
yesterday. Why did you not bring your

children with you this morning? I should be glad to see them."

"They are quite too noisy for a sick room," replied the visitor, "and my husband, who is the president of the Granville Bank, heard from Mr. Foster that you were a great invalid, and somewhat of a stranger in this part of the country. It is Eveline's birth-day, and she begged me to try and persuade you to let Comfort be among her guests."

"I am afraid that I shall have to disappoint her," said Mrs. Foster, "for my child has never been in any other house than this, and would feel very strangely away from home without her father or myself. What do you say, my darling? Would you be willing to go and see Mrs. Davis' little girls, with no one with you but Fanny?"

Comfort did not know what to answer, for she had a reason for wishing to see

7*

Mrs. Davis' children again, and yet she did not like to leave her mother. At length she said, "I don't know, mama, what is right. Won't you please think for me and tell me what to do?"

"I wished," said Mrs. Davis, "to take you home in my carriage to pass a few hours with my little girls. Your father would ride back with you this evening, and I hope that you would have a great deal to tell your mother when you re-turned."

"May I whisper to mama?" said Comfort, who felt that it would not be polite to do so without permission.

"Certainly, my child," replied Mrs. Davis, who was charmed with the nature and simplicity of all the little girl's words and actions.

Comfort clambered up to her mother's side, and putting her mouth close to her ear, said, "Mama, I have been wanting to see those little girls ever since Sunday. Perhaps if I tell them how good and kind our heavenly Father is, they won't grieve Him by acting so in His house again. You see they were not angry at what I said then, so they must be kind little girls, and would do right if they knew how. Perhaps their mother has never been sick, and you know you told me God had taught you many things by making you sick, that you would never have known if you were well."

While Comfort was whispering all this, Mrs. Davis watched her animated face, and thought she was one of the loveliest little beings that she had ever seen. Mrs. Foster had been afraid, at first, to let Comfort accept Mrs. Davis' invitation, but when she heard what was her object in wishing to do so, she felt that there was no fear that her simple faith would be perverted. "You may go, my darling," she said aloud, "but run quick and call Fanny, so as not to keep Mrs. Davis waiting. Tell her she can take you into her room to dress you, and that she must not be long about it."

Comfort kissed her mother affectionately, and did the same to Mrs. Davis, and then she went in search of Fanny, whom she found at the front door, staring at the carriage.

"What are you to wear, Miss Comfort?" exclaimed the nurse, with a puzzled air. "I am sure you have not got a thing that's fit to go to such a place in."

"Why, Fanny, what are you thinking about?" asked Comfort, opening her eyes in astonishment. "You know I have everything that's nice, and why should I care more about my clothes when I go to see Mrs. Davis, than when I stay at home. There is no being there greater than our heavenly Father, and no one certainly who loves me so well as mama."

"But," said Fanny, "didn't you see, Miss Comfort, how nice she was dressed?"

"Yes," said the little girl, very quietly, "and so were her children, but that's just the reason, maybe, why they don't think more about heaven, and I am glad I have no fine clothes if they would make me want to stay in this world away from the good God and my dear little sisters."

Fanny could not understand how anybody could be thankful that they had not beautiful things to wear, and she grumbled to herself all the while that she was dressing Comfort, because she was afraid that her darling would not look as well as the little people that she was going to meet.

When she had finished hooking the same blue dress that Comfort wore every day, and which she had only taken off to put on clean pantalettes, the little girl said eagerly, "Now, Fanny, please run in the garden and get me all the prettiest flowers that you can find. There are two or three sweet white jonquils, and ever so many white and blue violets." .

"Pray, Miss Comfort, what do you want of them?" asked Fanny, in astonish. ment.

"You'll see," said Comfort, looking very mysterious. When Fanny returned with the flowers, and some periwinkle that grew on the bank by the house, Comfort twisted them into two little wreaths, and put them inside of her white hat, just as she had seen some artificial flowers in the bonnets that Mrs. Davis' little children wore. "You see, Fanny," she said, "that I want to show those little girls how much prettier things are that God makes, than any others. You know He told us to look at the flowers of the field and see how beautiful they were, and that would teach us to. take no thought about our dress. These are sweet flowers, and anybody could not look at them without thinking that the finest clothes in the world were not half as beautiful."

As soon as Comfort went into her mother's room, Mrs. Foster noticed the new ornament in her little white hat, but she did not say anything about it, and Mrs. Davis only thought how sweetly the violets looked, peeping out among her golden curls. Comfort bade her mother good-bye, as if she were going away for a year, and Mrs. Foster could not help sighing as the bright little creature vanished from her sight.

CHAPTER V.

IT would be difficult to say whether Mrs. Davis or her little companion most enjoyed their drive to Granville, so much was that kind-hearted lady pleased with Comfort's remarks and evident delight at all that she saw and heard. It was the first time that the child had ever been in a carriage of any kind, and she felt almost as if they were flying over the ground, for the road was very smooth, and the horses knew that they were going home.   She was very much mortified when Mrs. Davis said, " Here we are," for it hardly seemed a moment since they started, and on Sunday, Granville had appeared quite a journey.   The house at which the carriage stopped, was a very handsome stone one, in the midst of a beautiful yard, filled with evergreens. There were no such trees near Mr. Foster's, and Comfort thought that they had put on their leaves before all their companions, and wondered what made them so early. Mrs. Davis told her that they were green all winter, and looked beautifully when they were covered with snow, and she picked off some of the long needle-shaped leaves, to show her how stiff they were, and what it was that made the brown carpet that covered the yard.

At that moment the door of the house opened, and a whole troop of little girls came running down the steps, all nicely dressed and looking very happy. Eveline Davis was the foremost, and she came right to her little visitor, and taking her by the hand, said,—

" Oh, I am so glad that you have

8

come; Mary said that she didn't believe
your mother would let you, but I was
almost sure that you would have your
own way."

"Oh, I can always do that," said Comfort, "for mama's way is my way, and
I want to do just what she tells me.
How happy you must be to live in such
a pretty place, where the trees are green
all the year! Do the birds build their
nests in these trees in the winter?"

"No, my darling," said Mrs. Davis,
smiling, "but I will show you a place
where they live all the year;" so saying,
she led Comfort around the porch to a
circular conservatory, which made a wing
on one side of the house, and opening
the glass door, told her to go in and see
her bird's nest.

Comfort did not need a second invita-
tation, for she had never seen such an
enchanting place. The glass roof was

so high, that some quite large trees which were planted in the earth in the centre of the green-house did not reach it, and some of these were both full of fruit and flowers at the same time. There were stands covered with beautiful and fragrant plants, all in blossom around the sides, and among those there were cages in which bright-colored birds were merrily singing.

"Here is my little canary's nest," said Mrs. Davis, calling Comfort to a cage which was hanging over some white hyacinths, that had just come out. Thus saying, she lifted the little girl up so that she could see the dearest little nest in the corner of the cage, in which there were two tiny birds with their mouths wide open, waiting to be fed. The mother was sitting on a perch over them, and had a little insect in her bill, with which she was going to feed one of them, and the male bird was singing at the top of the cage.

All the little girls who had followed Mrs. Davis into the conservatory, were loud in their expressions of delight, but Comfort stood looking at them in silence, with her blue eyes sparkling with pleasure. One of the visitors, named Anna Lathrop, asked, hesitatingly, whether canary birds liked to be shut up in a cage, and seemed quite relieved to hear that they were let out every morning, and always came back of their own accord.

"Oh, how much good it would do mama to come here!" exclaimed Comfort, at last. "Was not the garden of Eden just such a place, Mrs. Davis?"

"What makes you think so?" asked that lady, kindly.

"Because," answered Comfort, "you know that it had every kind of tree and flower, and mama told me that she thought it was always warm there, and there were blossoms and fruit at the same time, and that's just the way here. Oh, I wish I was Eve, and had a chance to try again whether I would be good!"

The little girls stared at Comfort, when she said this, and Mary Davis was so rude as to whisper to Jane Campbell,—

"I told you she was a queer little thing, and talked and acted just like an old woman."

Her mother did not hear this remark, but Anna Lathrop did, and she was afraid that Comfort might do the same, so she stepped up to her side, and putting her arm around her waist, said, affectionately,

"If you were Eve, I don't believe you would be naughty, and pick the fruit that you were forbidden to touch."

"I am afraid I should," said Comfort. "I did not think how easy it was to do

wrong when I said so. I have sometimes touched things that mother told
me to leave alone, and you know that
was just as bad."

"Oh, Mrs. Davis, do tell me what this
is," said a little girl named Etta Alston,
who was bending over a most singular
plant.

· "It is called the side-saddle flower,
and sometimes the pitcher-plant," replied Mrs. Davis, as the children all ran
to the spot. "That green cup holds
water for a great while, for the birds to
drink, and the lip of it is covered with
a kind of gum, so that the insects who
alight upon it cannot creep off, and sometimes many of them are drowned. There
is another kind, which has a lid to the
pitcher, and the water that it holds is
kept so clear that travellers drink it to
quench their thirst."

"How curious!" exclaimed Anna Lathrop. "Oh, here is such a strange plant! I just touched a leaf of it, and it shut right up, as if it were afraid of me. What made it do so, Mrs. Davis?"

"That is called a sensitive plant, and it always closes when it is touched, just as some little children become very still when a stranger speaks to them. But what ails my little Comfort? you are very silent, darling, are you tired?"

"Oh, no, ma'am," answered Comfort, looking up in her friend's face very gratefully, but still there was a sad expression upon her sweet countenance.

"What troubles you, then, my dear?" continued Mrs. Davis. "Tell me what you were thinking about, just as if I were your mama."

Comfort hesitated a moment, and then taking off her hat, untwined her little wreaths which she had fixed into it, and handed the fading, but still sweet violets,

to Mrs. Davis, saying, in a mournful tone
of voice,—

"They will be of no use."

The lady did not understand what
Comfort was thinking about, but imagined that on seeing so many beautiful
flowers, she had become discontented
with those which had before seemed to
her so pretty.

"Violets are always sweet," she said,
as she smelled the drooping flowers, "but
you shall take home a boquet of any
that you wish, to your mother; would
you like to do so?"

"Oh, yes," exclaimed Comfort, her
eyes dancing with joy; but a moment
after the same sober expression came
back to her face, and she added,—

"Indeed I was not thinking that I
wished for any prettier flowers than those
that grow at home. They always teach
me something, and I brought them to

show to your little girls, because I thought that they had never seen 'God's youngest children,' as mama calls them."

At these words the little girls crowded around the stranger, wondering what she was talking about, but they all looked kindly at her, excepting Mary Davis, who felt quite vexed that any one should think she was so ignorant.

"And what lesson have these little violets taught you, my rose-bud?" said Mrs. Davis, as she stooped to kiss the blushing cheek of the now embarrassed little girl.

At that moment, Comfort thought of something that her mother had once said about never being ashamed of anything that she thought or did, that was right. She felt, suddenly, as if her heavenly Father were standing right at her side, and saying, "Fear not, little one," so she looked up again with her usual trustful,

earnest air, and said frankly, "I will tell
you why I put these flowers in my hat
when I came here. Mama says that the
reason why she thinks so much about God
and heaven is because she is sick, and
that is why she talks about them to me
all the while. Your little girls did not
act on Sunday as if they knew what a
kind Father they had in heaven, and I
thought perhaps you had been so well
and so busy that you had not had time
to read His Book, or tell them what He
liked. But the flowers have taught me
almost as much as mama, and when I see
how quick they fade, and how pretty
they are, I think about the verse that
says the beauty of man must wither just
so, and of another that tells us to consider
them, and not think about our clothes.
I thought, that if Mary and Eveline could
see the pretty things that God makes,
they would not be proud of wearing fine

colors, and so I brought these flowers to
show them to-day. When I came here
and saw that they could look, every day,
at such beautiful plants and birds, and
yet did not love and praise Him, it
made me very sad, and I said to myself,
'It's no use showing my violets,' and I
couldn't think of any way to persuade
them that God was good."

This was a very long speech for little
Comfort to make, and when she got
through she cast down her eyelids, and
stood looking modest and thoughtful,
but not in the least ashamed. Mary
Davis took Jane Campbell by the arm,
and went out of the green-house, whispering to her, "I wish mother had left
that preaching little thing at home. We
don't behave any worse at church than
other children, but she seems to think
we are dreadful wicked just because we
laughed and talked a little."

But Eveline Davis did not follow her sister, for she was naturally a gentle, sweet child, and was really interested in what Comfort said. She put her arm around her neck, and whispered, "You shall teach me to be better, but, indeed, mama has often told us about what is right, but we are naughty children sometimes."

Comfort kissed her new friend warmly, and said eagerly, "Does your mother talk to you about such things? Well! I thought she must be a good lady. Now I know what mama meant, when she said good children honored their parents. If we don't do right, people think that nobody has taught us any better. Don't they, Eveline?"

"I am afraid they do," said the little girl, looking ashamed. "I never thought though, before, that any one would not know that mama was good, if I did not behave well. I will try and act so as to honor her more."

While the little girls were having this conversation, Anna Lathrop and Etta Alston were looking at a very curious cactus; and Mrs. Davis was telling them that the night-blooming cereus was of the same family, and how it inclosed its leaves in darkness and faded before daylight. They were very much interested in what she said, but they were interrupted by Mary Davis, who came back to the greenhouse, and called out, impatiently, "Do come and play, girls— we are not having any fun, at all. Jane wants to skip the rope; but I say, let us have a game of blind-man's-buff."

Comfort had never heard of either of these games before; and had never played with any children in her life; but she was ready to do just what pleased the rest, and Mrs. Davis proposed that they

9

should skip the rope, to suit Jane Campbell, in the piazza; and then she went in the house.

As Comfort did not know how to skip, she preferred to turn the rope; and Eveline took the other end, because she was the same height, while Jane and Mary stood together and went over it without tripping, till they were quite out of breath. Then Etta and Anna tried to do the same, but they were younger; and the first turn of the rope carried off one of Etta's little bronze slippers, and at the next attempt, it caught under Anna's chin.

When Comfort and Eveline had turned for others, till their arms were tired, Comfort tried to learn to skip; but her long gray pelisse caught at the first jump, and so Eveline proposed that she should go in the house and change it for a shawl of her own, which she offered to lend her. When they came back, they found that **Mary** Davis had been blind-folded; and the rest were waiting for them to make a ring round her, and play "Stero, stero, stop."

When the little circle had gone round three times, Mary called out, "Stop," and then pointing at Comfort with a stick, said, "Say Massachusetts." Comfort did not know that she was to try and conceal her voice, so she said "Massachusetts" very plain, and of course Mary knew who it was. Then Comfort was blinded, and it was a long time before she could guess who any of the children were, but at last she stopped at Eveline, and knew her voice. Soon after, **Mrs.** Davis called them into the house, and then they went into the dining-room to partake of Eveline's birth-day feast.

The table at which the children all sat down, did not look like any that Comfort had ever seen, for the dishes belonged to a new set which Eveline's father had just given her for a present, and many of them held beautiful confectionery and jelly that was as clear as amber. Comfort was so busy in admiring a little pyramid made of different colored candies, that she had forgotten that any of these pretty things were to be eaten till Mrs. Davis said,

"What will you have, my dear? The other children are all helped."

"Indeed I can't tell," replied Comfort, smiling, "for I don't know what you call these nice dishes, and I never tasted them. Won't you please to give me what you think best; I am sure they are all good."

"Oh, mama, give her some cream candy and some fruit cake," cried out Eveline, from the head of the table, where she was seated in honor of her birth-day.

"I know you'll like them, Comfort, for I always want to eat them till I am sick."

"Then, perhaps, I had- better not try them," answered Comfort, very simply, "for mama would feel troubled if I should not be well when I go home, and, besides, she thinks it is dreadful for little girls to make themselves sick eating. She told me one day that it was almost as bad as for men to drink too much."

"She is very right," said Mrs. Davis, "and I do not mean that you shall go home the worse for your visit. Here is a biscuit and some cold tongue, for you must be hungry after being in the air so long. When you have eaten that, I will give you some sponge cake, which will not hurt you, and Eveline will pick out some pretty mottoes and bon-bons for you to carry home."

Comfort thanked Mrs. Davis, and was

9*

quite contented with the choice she had made, but she thought to herself that it was very strange such a kind lady should have put anything on the table that was not good for little children. She wondered, too, what her mama would think of a little pile of good things by Jane Campbell's plate, for every time any thing was offered to the latter, she took some and laid it down as if she were afraid that she would not have another chance. All at once it entered her head that Jane was saving those things to give away, and she said, in a low voice, "Are you going to give these cakes and candies to some poor little girl who never has had any? If you are, she may have mine too that Mrs. Davis said she would give me to carry home."

Jane blushèd at this innocent remark, and muttered the words, "little simpleton," but Comfort did not know what she meant, and thought that was the name of some child for whom she had been heaping up nice things. Mrs. Davis, however, had heard the artless remark, and she thought it right to show Jane that she observed her rudeness, by saying, "Do you know any poor little girl, Comfort, who would like to taste such things?"

"I am not sure," said Comfort, "that I do, but there is one who plays in the lane behind our house, who never has any stockings or shoes, and once she came in the kitchen to ask for bread, and if she could not get enough of that, maybe she would like some cake. I think, though, she would like biscuit better, for mama says it is more healthy."

"How much that mother of hers must talk," whispered Mary Davis, who was sitting the other side of Jane Campbell. "I am afraid she will injure herself talking so much, for every other word is, ' mama says.' "

"For shame, Mary," said Eveline in a low tone, "she is my visitor, and you sha'n't treat her badly."

"Sha'n't, indeed," said Mary, aloud; "I should like to know who made you my mistress."

"What, quarrelling!" exclaimed Mrs. Davis, looking very much displeased. 'I am quite ashamed of you, Mary; if you cannot behave better, you must leave the table."

Mary made no reply, but she sat pouting till all the children had finished eating, and then she went out in the porch with Jane Campbell, and said she wished that hateful little Comfort Foster was where she came from, for that she had spoiled all her pleasure. Eveline now asked the rest of the children if they would like to see her books, and carried them to the nursery, where there was quite a little library.

Comfort had never dreamed that any body could be so rich, and did not know which of the pretty volumes to look at first. Eveline was much pleased by her sincere admiration, and said kindly,—

"Pick out any that you like, and I will lend them to you to read."

"Oh, how kind," exclaimed Comfort, and she fairly jumped up and down, and clapped her hands for joy. But the selection was no easy matter, for the books were very well chosen, and all looked so interesting, and were so full of pretty pictures, that Comfort was much more puzzled than she had been at dinner. She opened one, named "The Two Gardens," to see how she should like it, and became so interested that she forgot where she was, and felt as if she had been dreaming, when Eveline said, at last,—

"If you had rather read than play, Comfort, you can stay here with Hannah; she is our nurse, and will be very good to you, and I would stay myself, but mama would not like to have me leave my company."

This was a very tempting offer, but Comfort thought, I came here to see Eveline, and I ought to please her and not myself, so she laid down the book cheerfully, saying,—

"Oh, no! we'll go and play now, and then if your mother is willing I can read this pretty book to mama. It is about 'The Two Gardens' in the beginning and end of the Bible. Don't you wish that we were going to run about in those golden streets, and could see those beautiful gates of pearl?"

"Why, you must have been reading a fairy story," said Etta Alston. "I never saw anything like it in my Bible, and I say six verses at Sunday school every Sunday." '

"Oh, yes, there is," said Eveline, "for I have read it in the book Comfort has just laid down. If it was not in the Bible I should not believe there could be a pearl big enough to make a gate, for mama has what she calls a very large one, and it is only as big as her thumb nail."

"How I should like to see it," said Comfort, "I never saw a pearl."

" Well, let us come into mother's room, and I dare say she will show you all her jewels. Would you like to see them, Anna, and you, too, Etta ?"

Both the little girls declared that they should be delighted if Mrs. Davis would show them her ornaments, and as soon as Eveline told her mother what she wanted, the request was granted.

Etta tried the rings on to her fingers,

and Anna hoped that she would have
some when she had grown up, that were
like them, but Comfort was thinking of
something very different. When Eveline
spoke of her mother's jewels, she thought
of the text about the day "that God
should make up His jewels," and wondered what her heavenly Father could
think were as precious as men considered
these beautiful stones. She did not know
that human souls were called jewels by
that great and good Being, and that, perhaps, He gave them this name because
it cost so much to buy them. The little
girl thought that the large pearl was very
beautiful, for it looked so pure, and she
did not wonder that religion was called
the "goodly pearl." After she had tried
to imagine how a gate would look, just
as white and clear, she remembered that
she had read that the foundations of the
' new Jerusalem were made of precious.

stones, and she began to wonder whether
Mrs. Davis had any of the kind that
were mentioned. The only name that
she remembered was an emerald, and she
asked Mrs. Davis very politely if she had
any stone of that kind, and then Mrs.
Davis showed her a very beautiful green
one, which was set in a ring, and inquired how she came to think of it.
Comfort mentioned then how much she
liked to read about the beautiful city,
where her little brothers and sisters had
gone to live, and that she had often wondered how the precious stones looked
around the walls. Mrs. Davis had forgotten what the names of these stones
were, but she gave Comfort a Bible to
look for the place, and then looked to
see if she had any of the rest. Comfort was delighted when she showed her
a jasper, which was a yellow stone something like gold, and a topaz that was

10

more of an orange and very transparent, and a purple amethyst, set round with chrysolites.

"Oh, must not heaven be beautiful?" exclaimed Comfort, looking as if in imagination she saw the shining walls; "and just think, Harry and Kate have golden crowns and are always with God, and the Blessed Saviour."

Mrs. Davis wished that her own faith was as bright as that of the child, for she had once lost a little girl, and had the same reason for believing that she was an inhabitant of that beautiful city which Comfort loved so much to think about. Just as the jewel box was being closed, Comfort said,—

"Oh, please, stop a moment; you know that pretty thing that the high priest wore on his breast was made of jewels. Will you please find the place, and see if you have any of them. I don't know where it is, for I only read the chapters there that mama chooses."

Mrs. Davis could not turn directly to the place, but at length she found the verse with the names of the twelve stones, in each of which there was engraven the name of one of the tribes of Israel. She had five of the stones that were mentioned, and three were the same that were in the account of the beautiful city. The others were an agate and a diamond, but she did not even know what was the color of an onyx, or a carbuncle.

The other little girls had all become much interested in hearing about these precious stones, and wondered how it was that they did not find such interesting things in the Bible as their little companion. The time had passed so quickly, that they were very much surprised when a servant came and said that Mr. Foster was below, and the carriage was all ready, waiting to take Comfort home.

The moment that she heard her father's name, the little girl sprang to the door, and running down stairs, threw herself into his arms without ever noticing that there was anybody else in the room. Eveline followed as quickly as she could, with her little visitors, and Mrs. Davis, in a few moments, came after them with a paper of candies and bon bons in her hand, and some cakes for Comfort to give away.

"Oh, father, they are so kind to me!" said Comfort, as she seized the end of his ear-trumpet, "won't you thank them, and can't Eveline come and see me."

"Certainly, my dear, if Mrs. Davis will allow her to do so," said the delighted father; and then Mrs. Davis told him that his little daughter had behaved perfectly well, and that she should always be happy to see her; she then whispered to Eveline, who went out of the room and came back with a beautiful boquet, which was for Mrs. Foster, and then she sent for Mary, who had been off with Jane Campbell in another room, ever since the feast. Mary came in, looking very cross, but she did not dare to be rude again to Comfort, who asked her if she would not come and see her, and then Mr. Foster told her it was time to go. Mrs. Davis tied her hat, and put on the gray pelisse, and said, as she kissed her at parting, that she should love her almost as well as her own children.

10*

CHAPTER VI.

THE night after her visit to Granville, Comfort could not sleep. She turned over and over, till she grew so restless at last, that she called out, in a low voice,—

" Mama, mama !"

"What is it, my darling?" asked Mrs. Foster, who was awake, in an anxious voice.

" Oh, nothing, mama, only I cannot sleep, and I wanted to ask you not to let me go and see Mrs. Davis again."

" Why not ?" inquired Mrs. Foster, in surprise; "I thought that you had had a very pleasant day."

"So I had, mama, but when I came to say my prayers to-night, I could not think what I was about, and I don't feel right now. I don't understand it at all, mama dear."

"You are tired, my darling," said her mother, soothingly, "go to sleep, and to-morrow you will think differently."

"But, mama, as soon as I close my eyes, instead of thinking about seeing the beautiful city, I imagine that you and I are living in a house like Mrs. Davis, with all those pretty flowers, and a library full of nice books, like those Eveline showed me. Is it right to go anywhere that makes us think less of heaven, mama?"

"Certainly not, my child, if we can help it, but if we carry a pure heart every where, no place can do us any harm."

"Then I am afraid that my heart is not pure," replied Comfort, in a very sorrowful tone, for she had often heard her mama say, that the pure in heart should see God.

"Then, dearest," said her mother, tenderly, "you can ask your heavenly Father to make it so, and when you have done this, try and go to sleep."

Comfort did as her mother told her, and in a few moments she was dreaming that she was walking with her sister Kate and Eveline Davis in one of the golden streets of the new Jerusalem, and Eveline had on a crown, set with diamonds, while her own had one great pearl in the middle of it, and around the border were engraved the words, "Blessed are the pure in heart." The trees that they saw were much more beautiful than those in the conservatory, and birds of every color were building nests in their branches, and fruit hung on all the boughs as clear as crystal and delicious in taste. But the most beautiful thing in this lovely place was a throne of gold, on which sat a Being that looked as the little girl had often pictured her Saviour, and He was saying, in a very gentle voice, "Suffer little children to come unto me and forbid them not."

The whole dream was a very sweet one, and such as no child could have had who had not very often thought about such things in her waking hours. All the next day, Comfort kept going over it in her mind, and wondering whether heaven would really be as beautiful as that vision. When she was going to bed she came to her mother and said, "I don't think, mama, that my visit did me any harm, for I have hardly thought of it to-day, only to be thankful that everybody was so kind, and that I saw so many pretty things. Don't you think that God heard my prayer, mama, and made my heart more pure?"

"I hope so, dearest, and if you try to keep it clean, He will always help you."

"And did He send me that lovely dream, mama, to make me remember that nothing in this world can ever be half as pretty as what we shall see in heaven?"

"Perhaps so, my darling. He will always find some way of teaching His children, and if your thoughts during the day are full of holy things, your dreams will be like them. Good night, darling. Go to sleep now, and perhaps you may again dream of the beautiful city."

A few weeks after this conversation, Mrs. Foster's health began to improve, and Comfort, to her great delight, saw her mother sitting for half an hour every day, in the large easy-chair which was her father's favorite seat. A sorrowful heart had made Mrs. Foster more ill than she would otherwise have been, but the pleasure of again talking to her husband, and the happiness that she found in the society of her dear little girl, soon worked wonders. Comfort was quite sure that the improvement in her mother's health was an answer to the prayer which her father made every morning, and so it was, by whatever means it might have been brought about. Mrs. Davis had called, once or twice, to see the invalid, and when she found that she was sitting up, insisted that whenever she was able to go out, she should send for her carriage and take a short drive. This was a delightful idea to Comfort, who was the happiest little creature alive at the very thought of her mother's recovery, but Mrs. Foster was not yet strong enough to walk across the room, so she told her little girl that she must be very patient and not expect her to be well too soon.

The first time that Mrs. Davis came

to see them after Eveline's birth-day, she brought a number of books that Comfort had particularly liked, and told her that Eveline had sent them to her as a present. Mrs. Foster told her little ·girl that she might accept them, and for many days Comfort spent all her mornings in reading these treasures aloud to her mother, and when she came to the last one she looked very sorrowful and said, "What shall I do now, mama, I have nothing more to read."

"Nothing?" repeated her mother, in an inquiring tone, and laid her hand on the books which always stood on her little table.

"Oh, mama, I meant no story-book. I know what you mean; you think I have not liked to read the Bible so much since I have had the books that Eveline sent me. I don't think it has seemed so interesting, and yet all the stories we have been reading are about being good."

"I know it, my dear, but they have so much in them that is amusing, that sometimes one almost forgets what they were meant to teach. You have been more anxious to know what happened to poor little Willy Newton, than whether he was ever cured of his faults."

"So I have, mama," said Comfort, with her usual candor. "I had not even thought what I was to learn from the book. I am glad, now, that I have not a library full like Eveline, or I should be always reading for the story."

"I will tell you what we can do to occupy ourselves," said Mrs. Foster. "Little girls have to learn a great deal while they are young, and generally go to school, but I shall try and teach you myself, now that I am so much better. One of the first studies that children have to go through is that which is called geo-graphy."

"And what is that, mama?" asked Comfort, for her knowledge about very common things was much less than what she possessed with regard to the Bible.

"Geography," replied her mother, "is a description of the world in which we live. You know you asked why Mrs. Davis smiled when you wanted to know if she had been to Jerusalem, and thought that she could ride there, and you were astonished to learn how many thousand miles you would have to travel before you could reach the Holy Land. If you had studied geography you would have known better."

"Oh, mama! how I shall like to learn it!" exclaimed Comfort, her eyes spar-kling with pleasure. "Can't we begin this morning?"

"We have no books, dearest, that are

simple enough for you to understand;
but stop! I have thought of a plan; what
country would you like to learn about
first ?"

"Oh, the one where our Saviour lived,"
answered Comfort, eagerly.

"Well, then, darling, draw that little
table nearer to my chair, and open the
Bible on it, to the map in the beginning
—I mean what you used to call the empty
picture."

Comfort fixed the table and the book
as her mother told her, and then Mrs.
Foster said,—

"We will take the mountains in Pales-
tine first. A mountain, you know, is
a very high piece of land, like that which
you see behind this house in the distance.
Now, tell me in what mountain the Ark
rested after the flood?"

"I don't know, mama, only the name
begins with an A, and is a hard one."

"Well, find it, darling, and then I will show it to you on the map."

Comfort soon found the place, for she knew that it was in the beginning of Genesis, and then her mother showed her where mount Ararat was situated, and that it was not in Judea, but in a country to the south of it, that we now call Arabia.

The little girl listened very attentively to what Mrs. Foster said, and when she had done, asked very eagerly, if Arabia was not a part of America. Her mother smiled at this question, and said, kindly,

"I forgot, my darling, that you did not know anything about the great divisions of the world. We must begin a little farther back in our study." Then she rang the bell for Fanny, and told her to see if she could find a globe anywhere, which they had brought with them from Canada. When the nurse understood what was wanted, she went up in the garret and unpacked a large box which had not been opened for many years, and there she found two globes, one for teaching geography, and the other astronomy. As she did not know what Mrs. Foster wished, she brought both down.

"Oh, mama, here are two worlds," exclaimed Comfort, as she knelt down on the floor by them, and tried to turn them round with her little hands.

"This is the one we live in, because I see the name America. Is the other the sun, or the moon?"

"Neither, my darling," replied Mrs. Foster. "Don't you see it is covered with little spots? These are the stars, and by and by you shall learn all about them."

"Oh, oh, how delightful!" shouted Comfort, in a perfect ecstasy, as she ran from one globe to the other, without being able to tell which interested her most.

Mrs. Foster then asked Fanny to put the terrestrial globe, that is, the one which represented the earth, upon a chair by her side, and Comfort stood by it while her mother explained the first chapter of Genesis. The little girl could not at first realize that she was standing on the outside of a great round world, that was moving over and over, every day, but she had been accustomed to believe a great many things that she did not understand, so that she had no doubt that what her mother told her was true. When she heard that this world had once been all a dark mass, without any shape, and entirely empty, she realized how much power was necessary to change it into the beautiful home in which she now lived.

Mrs. Foster described the light as it

shone out when God said "Let there be light," and then how the clouds formed in the sky, and left the water covering all the outside of the earth.

"Now," she said, "we shall have use for our globe; we will try and imagine it all covered with water as it was at the beginning of the third day, when God said, 'Let the dry land appear, and God called the dry land earth, and the gathering together of the water called He seas.' All those dark spots with three or four black lines around the edge, represent water. There are five of these great bodies of water named oceans, and they are all connected together. These at the top and bottom of the globe are called the Northern and Southern Oceans; the broad one in the middle is the Pacific Ocean, and in some places it is seven thousand miles wide; the narrow one is the Atlantic, and there is another flowing between the Pacific and Atlantic, and that is called the Indian Ocean."

While Mrs. Foster was speaking, Comfort hardly turned her eyes from the globe, and spelt the names of all the oceans that she had pointed out, but now she asked her mother if she would answer a question that had just come into her head.

"I have been thinking," she said, "that when the flood came, it must have covered all the dry land up, for you know you told me that the water was a great many feet deep all over the earth. Now, mama, when the flood went down, did the water run back into all the same places which had been seas in the beginning?"

"You have asked me rather a hard question," replied Mrs. Foster, with a smile, "and one that I cannot answer; so I think, instead of imagining the world

after the creation, we shall have to take
it as it has been since the flood went
down. On the other side of the globe,
there is a long piece of land almost
separated in the middle, which is called
North and South America. We will
not turn it up, for in old times no one
knew that there was such a country.
Now, see, Europe, Asia, and Africa. If
you wanted to choose a place which could
be reached most easily by the inhabitants
of all these countries, which would you
take ?"

Comfort looked very carefully at these
three great divisions of the earth, and
saw that the Red Sea separated Asia from
Africa, and that the Black Sea was between Europe and Asia, and the Medi-
terranean Sea between Europe and Africa.

"Mama," she said, at length, putting
her hand on the country that we now
call Turkey in Asia, "would it not be

easy for the people in Europe, and those of Asia and Africa, to meet here? It seems to me as if this spot was the nearest to all three countries."

Mrs. Foster was delighted with the quickness of her little scholar, and put her hand fondly on her head, saying, "You are right, my darling; Judea was in that very place, because God wanted to have the nation who served Him, and the birth-place of His Son, where all the world, that was then known, could hear of them. Travellers from all countries came to this spot in the time of the Apostles. Don't you remember all those nations, with hard names, who were gathered together at Jerusalem, when the Apostles received the Holy Ghost?"

"Oh yes, mama, and how Peter could speak all their languages, and how they went home telling what they had seen. I shall not forget where Judea was."

" Well, then, now we will go on with
the mountains mentioned in the Bible,
most of which are in the country that
I have just told you is now called Turkey
in Asia. But you have been listening
so attentively that I am afraid you are
tired now, so perhaps we had better wait
till to-morrow."

Comfort was almost sure that she was
not wearied, but her mother remembered
that it had been thought that little Kate's
health was injured by the activity of her
mind, so she told Fanny to put the globe
up on the bureau, and then take Comfort
out to walk.

We have forgotten to mention that Mr.
Foster had been obliged, by business, to
leave home for several weeks, and his
little daughter had never been to church
again on that account. Mrs. Foster was
able only to write a few lines, at the
time, to her husband, so he knew very

little of what was going on at home.
Comfort was exceedingly desirous to
write a letter herself, but she had only
just begun making letters on the slate,
and it was hard to tell what they were
intended for, but now she had a motive
to learn, and improved very fast. One
day, she came to her mother, who was
sitting up and writing a short letter, and
said, "Mama, just see if you can read
the word on my slate."

"'Comfort Foster;' is not that it?"
asked her mother, encouragingly.

"Oh, you read it, didn't you, mama?
Now let me see if I cannot write another
word."

Comfort sat down on the floor again,
with her slate in her lap, and an old
sampler from which she had been copy-
ing the writing letters before her, because
she did not wish to trouble her mother
to make a copy while she was busy.

"There! there!" she exclaimed, almost dancing with joy at her own success, as she again handed the slate to her mother.

"'Come home, dear papa.' Why, at this rate, you will soon learn to write a letter. Write as much as you can on your slate, and when I have done I will give you a lead pencil and you shall put it down at the bottom of my letter."

This was charming. Comfort washed her slate all clean, and then she ruled it as nicely as she could, with a book, and began what she called a letter, though she had never read one, only in books, in her life, for Mr. Foster's epistles had been on business, though they always contained some message for his dear little girl. By the aid of the sampler, and the letters that she had already learned, Comfort made out to write the following note to her papa :—

" Come home, dear papa, God is making mama well, because three prayed for her, you, and Fanny, and I.   I learn all about the earth ; won't you bring me a book to study more about it?   Mrs. Waddle has got the pip.   I want to go to church again.   Mama is going to ride in a carriage, when she gets better.   I wish your ear-trumpet was long enough for one end to reach here.   I ask God to take care of you, every night, and bring you home safe."   Your little daughter,

COMFORT FOSTER.

When Comfort had done writing this letter, she found, to her surprise, that her mother had gone back to bed, for she had been so much engaged that she did not hear her move at all.   Many little girls would have fretted at being obliged to wait a whole day before they could finish their letter, but Comfort never dreamed of doing such a thing. She set up her slate carefully, where what she had written would not get rubbed out, and then she sat down by her mother's bed, and read to her in a low, gentle voice, till Mrs. Foster fell fast asleep.

The next day, Comfort was allowed to copy her letter, and though the capital letters were not in the right place, all the words were properly spelt, and Mr. Foster thought, when he received it, that it was very nicely written for a little girl of Comfort's age. About a week after, he came home, and the moment that Comfort heard his step in the yard, she knew it and ran to meet him. He took her up in his arms and kissed her fondly, and then carried her up into her mother's room. His surprise was great when he saw his dear wife sitting up, and looking better than she had done for many years. Comfort was contented to remain silent upon his knee, while he told her mother all about his journey, and heard the history of what had happened during his absence. Before he had learned half that he wished, Fanny came to say that tea was ready, and the little girl was very happy to be seated once more at the table with her father, for during his absence she had been obliged to have her breakfast all alone, and her tea too, when her mother was tired, or asleep, as she often was at that hour.

After tea, Mr. Foster told Fanny to bring his portmanteau into the dining-room, and there he unpacked it and took out an air-pillow which he had brought for his wife, who complained most of the heat in her head, and also a nice dressing-gown, the pattern of which Comfort particularly admired. She did not say, " What have you got for me, papa?" or even think of herself, so much oc-

cupied was she with the idea of her
mother being made more comfortable;
but Mr. Foster had by no means forgotten his little daughter. He drew from
his portmanteau a large paper parcel,
and then telling Fanny to bring the
things he had taken out into Mrs. Foster's
room, he went up there himself, followed
by Comfort, who was trying to make
herself useful by carrying a light package which Fanny had dropped. Mrs.
Foster was much pleased with her husband's thoughtfulness in bringing her
such a nice cool pillow, and she let Comfort try and blow it up, but the little
girl got quite out of breath before it was
half full of air. Mrs. Foster thought, too,
that her new dressing-gown was particularly pretty, and did not say anything
because it was not black, for she saw
that Mr. Foster wished that she should
wear mourning no longer.

12*

"And here, my little Comfort," said Mr. Foster, as he undid the package that he had brought up stairs, "is a geography and writing-book for you, and a volume of poetry, with a hymn in it for every day in the year."

"Oh, papa, how kind! what can I give you; I have nothing but kisses, but you shall have plenty of them," cried the little girl, kissing him again and again.

"There, that'll do," said Mr. Foster, laughing, "you must stop, or I can't show you what else I have brought. Here is a dissected map of America, and when you have learned the geography you can put it together."

Comfort had never heard of such a thing before, but she did not doubt that it would be a delightful occupation to try and make the map, but the last present which her father had brought put all the rest out of her mind. This was a very neat Prayer Book for her to carry to church, and a Testament, so small that she could have it always in her pocket, and for that purpose it was slipped into a little case. Comfort had so often wished that her mother's Bible was not so big, and the one out of which her father read was almost as heavy. Since summer had come, she was very fond of sitting out under the trees, or in the wood behind the house, and many times she had thought how she should like to read some of her favorite passages of Scripture, with the birds singing around her, and the sweet air fanning her face.

She had hardly begun to express her delight at all these new treasures, when Mrs. Foster reminded her that it was time for her to be undressed; but she laid them quietly by, only asking a few moments to get her mind quiet before she said her prayers, so that she might remember all the things for which she ought to thank her heavenly Father. Her father's return; the book out of which she could learn more of the beautiful world that God had made; the little Testament that she could have always with her to remind her of His presence and the love which, from her birth, had been so mindful of all her wants, were each mentioned in her simple address to that beloved Friend, who became dearer at every step in life.

With one more kiss from her father and mother, Comfort went to rest, and though there was talking in the room, she was not kept awake, for she fixed her mind on the subject which was always the last in her thoughts at night, and so she fell asleep.

CHAPTER VII.

THE Sunday after Mr. Foster's return, he told Comfort that she might again go with him to church. The little girl was even more delighted at this permission than she had been before, for she knew now exactly what a church was, and that it was a blessed privilege to worship God in an assembly of Christians.

As it was a very warm day, her mother told Fanny to take out a thin, white muslin dress which Kate used to wear, and see if Comfort had not out-grown it. She was pleased to find that it was just the right length, and as it was made like an infant's dress, with ribbons run in around the waist and neck, it could be drawn up to fit the little girl very nicely. The material of the dress was a fine dotted muslin, which Mrs. Foster had cut up for clothes for her children, as after she lost the first little boy, she had always worn mourning, and never thought that she should leave it off again. Comfort, however, did not seem to perceive that the dress was any nicer than the cambric ones which she wore every day, only she said,—

"Oh, how cool this will be, and I am so glad that I am to wear white to church, for you know, mama, you told me that the minister wore his surplice as a sign of purity, and I think it would be very nice if all the people had on white too."

"But you must remember, my darling, that it is a pure heart which God likes best, and what our Saviour said to the Pharisees who were so particular about washing."

"I will try and not forget it," said Comfort, **very** meekly, and then there was not time for any more conversation. Fanny brought out a round straw hat, which she tied under the little girl's chin with blue strings, and her mama put a handkerchief around her neck, so that the sun might not burn it where the curls did not cover it, and then she was all ready for church.

"You will not need my Prayer Book," said her mother, "but you had better put yours in your pocket, and your little Testament too, if you wish to find the lessons, for I am afraid that your warm little hands will soil them, and I am not sure that the color may not come out of your mits, so you had better take them off in church. If you are uncomfortable, you can lay aside your hat and this handkerchief, but do it quietly, my dear, before the service commences. Your father

has gone down stairs, so give me a kiss
and run after him."

"Oh, mama," said Comfort, as she bid
her good morning, "how nice it is to
leave you sitting up here instead of in
bed, as you were when we went to church
before. If we keep on praying for you,
I am sure that God will make you quite
well."

The walk to Granville, that morning,
seemed quite long, and Comfort was very
tired, but she did not mind that, because
she thought about the place to which
she was going. Neither did she tell her
father that she was weary, for she was
sure that he would then insist on carrying her part of the way, and she knew
that she was now very heavy. To make
the time seem shorter, she repeated over
a number of hymns, and her catechism,
for Mr. Foster did not seem inclined to
talk, for his mind was full of very serious

reflections. "This walk," thought Comfort to herself, "makes me think of what mama said about its being no matter what sort of a life we had, if we only reached heaven at last." At this moment they came to the top of a hill from which they could see the church, and Comfort immediately remembered the hymn,

"As when the weary traveller gains
    The height of some commanding hill,
His heart revives, if o'er the plains
    He sees his home, though distant still,"

and she could understand why life was so much pleasanter after the dream in which she saw the beautiful city so plainly.

The church bell was ringing when Mr. Foster and his little girl entered the door, and as Mrs. Davis had invited them always to sit with her, they again went into her seat, and, soon after, she entered with her two little girls. Com-

13

fort returned the greeting of her companions only by a pleasant smile, and, as she was very warm, took off her hat and handkerchief, and laid her mits with them under the seat, where they would not be in the way of any one. Then, she drew out her Prayer Book, and was busy in finding the place till the organ began to play. Though Mrs. Foster had explained to the little girl that the music was made by an instrument and not by the angels, it still sounded very sweet, and prepared her mind for the services.

After the sermon was finished, the clergyman came down from the pulpit, and, standing in the chancel, invited all the children who were present, to come forward and be catechised. Comfort had never heard of such a thing before, and did not know what she was to do, for her father was so deaf that, of course, he did not hear the announcement, and she could not think of any way of making him understand what she wished. But Mary and Eveline Davis rose from their seats and passed out of the pew, and then Mr. Foster thought what must be going on, and whispered to Comfort that she might go and be catechised too.

When the little girl reached the chancel, the clergyman looked at her with much interest, for she had not remembered to put her hat on, and he thought her one of the loveliest looking children that he had ever seen, with her sweet, earnest face shaded by those long golden curls, and her little delicate figure dressed in such a pure, childlike garment. She had taken her place at the corner of the chancel, and when he asked what was her name, and she answered, "Comfort," he thought that must be some pet name, and said, kindly, "I mean the name by which you were baptized, **my** child."

"Comfort, sir," the little girl repeated, with the same sweet unembarrassed voice, while her mild blue eyes were fixed upon his face with the most reverential expression.

The clergyman passed on to the next child with the question, "Who gave you this name?" and when he came round again to Comfort, asked, "What is your duty to God?" adding, "However, that is a long answer for such a little girl, and perhaps you cannot say it all."

Comfort felt as if she were reciting her catechism in the immediate presence of God, her heavenly Father, and her manner therefore was very solemn when she answered this question, and the words "with all my heart, and all my mind, and all my strength," were spoken so earnestly that the clergyman wondered who had taught the child the meaning of the words that she spoke.

"And why is this your duty to God, my dear? I mean, why should you love Him so much?" he asked.

"Because He is our best Friend, and loves us, and made us, and died for us," said Comfort, with much animation.

"How do you know that He loves us?" asked the clergyman, who was much interested in the manner in which his last question had been answered.

"Because mama says so, and I read it in my little Testament. I will show you the place, sir."

So saying, Comfort drew her Testament from her pocket, and, turning to the text, "We love Him because He first loved us," read it aloud in a low, but very distinct voice.

Poor Mr. Foster could not hear a word that his child said, but he saw that the

13*

minister looked pleased whenever he came to her, and was not afraid of her saying anything wrong. "Out of the abundance of the heart the mouth speaketh," and he knew that his little daughter's heart was full of good desires and holy thoughts.

After the catechism was all repeated, the clergyman made a few remarks, and then he told the children to kneel around the chancel while he offered the concluding prayer and benediction.

Comfort felt as if she were a step nearer to God, as she knelt where she had read in the Prayer Book that persons were confirmed and partook of the Lord's Supper. After the benediction was pronounced, she thanked God for letting His minister hear her say her catechism, and asked for strength to remember and practice what he had said, and then she prayed that, when she was old enough, she might come to that place to repeat the vows that had been made at her baptism, and to receive the precious sacrament.

The little girl was so absorbed in her devotions, 'that she did not hear the children all going to their seats, and was surprised, when she rose, to find that they were gone, and the people were leaving church. The minister still stood in the chancel, and, coming towards her, said kindly, as he saw her bewildered expression, " Whose Comfort are you, my little darling ?"

" My father's and mother's," she replied with great simplicity.

"I am sure of that, but what is their name, and who brought you here ?"

" My father, and he is called Mr. Foster. How can I get to him, sir ?"

" Wait for me a moment, and I will help you find him," said the clergyman;

and then he went into the vestry room, leaving Comfort standing alone by the chancel. She was not at all afraid, however, and as soon as the people left the church she saw her father coming up the aisle, and, at the same time, the minister came out of the vestry room.

"This is my father, sir," she said, as she took hold of Mr. Foster's hand. "He is deaf, and cannot hear what you say, but if you will come to see us you can talk to him through his ear-trumpet, and I know my sick mama will like to have you come."

Mr. Harrington—for that was the minister's name—said he would be very happy to pay Mr. Foster a visit, and then Comfort made signs to explain to her father that she had been asking the clergyman to come and talk to him through his ear-trumpet.

Mr. Foster repeated the little girl's

invitation, and said that his deafness had kept him at home for a long time, but that now he hoped to attend church regularly, and to be considered a member of the parish.

The clergyman and her father continued talking, as they walked down the aisle, though in a low tone and serious manner, and when they parted, Comfort heard Mr. Harrington say, "I will try and ride out some morning to breakfast with you," and she felt so thankful that their house was to be honored by a visit from a minister of God.

CHAPTER VIII.

A few days after the catechising in church, Mrs. Davis called to see if Mrs. Foster was not well enough to take a short drive, and brought her two chil-dren, at the same time, to pay a visit to Comfort. The parlor had been aired and dusted since the first time that Mrs. Davis came, but it was still kept dark. Fanny, however, unbolted the shutters, after asking the guests to seat themselves, which they did by the sense of feeling, and then she went to see if her mistress was able to receive them in her chamber.

As soon as the nurse was out of hear ing, Mary got up and walked around the room, staring at the faded, old fashioned furniture, and examining con temptuously a picture worked in satin which was hanging over the fire-place. It was the last piece of needlework that Mrs. Foster had done, and represented a tomb beneath a willow tree, over which a female form was bending with a very sorrowful expression. There was no name upon the monument, but a branch of a rosé tree with four buds broken off, and the two blossoms which were standing had a yellow and withered appearance. · A harp stood in the corner of the room, but three of the strings were broken, and the gilt which ornamented the frame was tarnished by dampness and want of care.

"What a gloomy looking place!" exclaimed Mary, when she had completed her survey. "Pray take us to ride with Mrs. Foster, for I shall die if I have to stay here with that prosy little Comfort."

"Why did you come, Mary?" asked

her mother, in a displeased tone. "You knew that Mrs. Foster had been an invalid for many years, and that your only amusement would be the society of her dear little girl."

"Well, it was very foolish in me," replied Mary, pouting, "but I was anxious to see what kind of a place that queer young one came out of. I can't imagine, mother, what makes you want us to associate with such people."

Mrs. Davis did not take any notice of the impertinent tone in which those words were spoken, but replied in rather a sad voice,—

"My reason is, Mary, because I think you may, perhaps, learn from that sweet child to behave in such a way as to be some comfort to your mother."

Eveline had said nothing, but she, too, had been thinking that it would be dreadful to live in such a dull, quiet place. The manner in which her mother spoke, touched her heart, and going to her side, she said, soothingly,—

"I will try, mama, and learn to be better. If Mary don't wish to stay here while you are out with Mrs. Foster, I shall not mind her going at all."

"But I should, very much," replied Mrs. Davis, "for she would be sure to hurt Mrs. Foster's feelings by some rude remark. Now that she has come, she must do as I wish, and I shall be extremely displeased if she does anything to pain her little friend. At this moment a light step was heard on the stairs, and then a fairy-like form sprang into the room, and Comfort flew from one to the other, exclaiming,—

"I am so glad you have come. Mama is better, Mrs. Davis, and she thinks that she will be able to go with you. Fanny is dressing her, and then she and Jane

14

will bring her down stairs and put her in the carriage, so she won't trouble you to come up."

"I am delighted to hear it," replied Mrs. Davis, "and I am going to leave Mary and Eveline with you while she is gone, if you would like their company."

"Oh, that will be so nice, won't it, Eveline?" exclaimed Comfort. "We can play in mama's room, and I have wanted to see you so much. Do you like cats and chickens?" she added, turning to Mary, who looked as disagreeable as she well could.

"I like cats in the cellar, to kill rats, and chickens on the table to eat," she replied, in a tone that was barely civil.

Comfort was so kind herself that she never dreamed that this could be said to annoy her, and answered, merrily,—

"What a funny taste! I should not

like my cat, Rosa, at all, if I saw her eating up a pretty little mouse, and Toppy is much more beautiful with his white crest on his head than he would be roasted for dinner. But won't you excuse me while I run and help mama down?"

Mrs. Davis smiled at the idea of Comfort's being any assistance, but the little girl felt as if she was much older and stronger than she really was, and offered to take hold of the arm-chair, in which she found her mother seated, so as to help Fanny and Jane.

"Run away, darling," said Mrs. Foster, "I am afraid you will get knocked over, yourself. Get me my work-bag out of the drawer, at the bottom of the bureau, and put a pocket handkerchief and my bottle of salts in it; and then take my air-pillow down stairs, for that is light enough for you to carry."

Comfort was pleased to be thus made of use, and stood at the bottom of the stairs, holding her mother's pillow when the invalid arrived there in safety.

Mary and Eveline Davis ran out in the hall, for they were very anxious to see the mama that Comfort was talking about, but her pale face was hidden by a thick green veil, and they only saw a very old-fashioned black bonnet, and a heap of grayish-black clothes, carried between a fat, untidy-looking cook, and the equally uncouth nurse.

"So that's your mother?" said Mary, in a contemptuous tone, as Mrs. Foster was borne out into the yard, whither Mrs. Davis followed her.

The tone in which these words were spoken, could not escape even Comfort's unsuspecting ear. She turned quickly round, and looked in Mary's face, with a mingled expression of wonder and reproach, and the tears filled her soft eyes as she answered, mildly,—

"Yes! that is my mother, my blessed mother!"

The heartfelt love with which these words were uttered, touched Eveline's feelings. She put both arms around Comfort's neck, and whispered to her,—

"I know she is a dear sweet woman though we couldn't see her face, and I wish she would teach me to be just like you."

"Oh it wouldn't do to have two alike," replied Comfort, the smile coming back to the face, "you know there are not ever two leaves alike. Did you ever try to find them, Mary?"

"No!" said Mary, who was a little subdued by the mild reproach conveyed in the answer which Comfort had made to her last rude remark. "I am sure, though, that I have seen a great many

14*

leaves in which there was not the least difference. I will show you two in a moment."

The children then ran out in the yard, and hunted under the poplars for a long time, to find two leaves that were precisely similar, but their search was vain. When the shape and color was alike, the little thread-like frame-work of the leaves was different, so they gave up in despair, and went to looking for four-leaved clover. While thus engaged, Comfort's pretty cat came purring after her mistress. The little girl took her up in her arms, and said triumphantly,—

"Now look at her, Mary, and see if you don't think her mouth is too white and sweet to be eating rats and mice?"

"That is what she was made for," replied Mary, scarcely noticing the graceful animal, but Eveline smoothed her soft fur, and said she had never seen such a pretty cat, and that she guessed she was a queen, and not meant to live like common cats.

The sun was getting so warm, that it drove the little ones into the house, and then Comfort took them up into her mother's room, which she thought was such a delightful place. She asked Mary if she would like to play with her dissected map, but the discontented visitor wished to do nothing that would please her kind entertainer. She sat sulkily staring around the room, excepting when she got up and examined some little article which was lying on the bureau or table, which she laid down again with a most contemptuous expression.

Comfort began to think that Mary was tired, and wanted to be let alone, so she turned her attention to Eveline, and then they were very happy together. Eveline was amused with the description

Comfort gave of the way that she spent her mornings, and when she heard that she could write, proposed that they should open a correspondence.

"Your papa will bring your letters to town and give them to me, and I will send an answer in the same way. Won't that be nice?"

Comfort thought it would be very nice indeed, and almost the same as if they lived together. She told Eveline about her little sister, and how often she had wished for some one to play with and to talk to, and that now, she should never feel lonely.

"But no," she added, "I don't really feel lonely ever, for mama is such pleasant company; only sometimes when she is asleep, or wants to be still, and papa is not at home, then I wish I had a little sister."

By and by the conversation turned

upon the catechising, and Eveline said,—

"How dared you speak up so to the minister? I was frightened almost to death, when it came my turn to answer."

"What were you afraid of?" asked Comfort, in surprise.

"Why all the people who were looking on, and heard us; were you not afraid of them?"

"Oh, no!" answered Comfort; "I never thought about there being anybody in church but the clergyman and ourselves; I mean any human beings, for I felt as if our heavenly Father was in our midst, and hearing every answer."

"I am sure that would have frightened me," replied Eveline. "I can't imagine how you can be so bright and happy, when you think so much about serious things. Sometimes, at night, after I go to bed, it comes into my head that God is everywhere, and it makes me so miserable that I get up and call Hannah to come and sit by me till I fall asleep."

"I am so sorry for you," said Comfort, in a very sad tone. "Anybody must be so unhappy that don't like to think that God is with them, for you know we can't get out of His sight for a single. moment."

"Oh! don't say so," said Eveline, closing her eyes, as if to shut out her Creator from her thoughts; "I can't bear to think of it."

"But, dear Eveline," replied Comfort, soothingly, "why do you feel so about our best and kindest Friend? He loves us better than our mothers, and does everything to make us happy."

"But I can't imagine anybody that I have never seen, and love them," said Eveline. "I know how mama looks, but I don't know what God is like, and I am so afraid of Him."

"Don't you remember," said Comfort, earnestly, "that our Blessed Saviour is God, and that He became man? Can't you imagine a man like our Saviour, looking sweeter and kinder than any man you ever saw? That's the way I do when I get puzzled, and now I always see the same face, and, oh, it is so beautiful!" and Comfort's eyes grew bright as if the vision of her Saviour was present in all its loveliness and sacredness.

Mary, who had been listening to the conversation, though she pretended not to hear it, was astonished at the expression of the little girl's face, and wondered why it was that she was so different from all the children she had ever known.

There was a moment of silence, in which Comfort and Eveline both appeared to be thinking deeply, and then

Comfort said, very earnestly, to her dear companion,—

"Dear Eveline, I have thought of the reason why you may be so troubled. The Bible says 'the pure in heart shall see God.' Perhaps if you were to ask Him to make your heart pure, by and by you would feel that He was near, and begin to see Him as He is; I mean He would come before you as a dear, kind Friend, who loves you, and then you would never be tired of thinking of Him."

"I never said any such prayer," replied Eveline. "There is not any such in our little book."

"Well, can't you say to our heavenly Father, 'Please to give me a pure heart?' That is what I say every night."

"I don't know; I never said a prayer that was not in a book," said Eveline, despondingly. "But couldn't you say it for me?"

"Oh yes, I will, every night, but that won't do any good, unless you say it yourself too. Do try, Eveline."

The sound of carriage wheels was now heard, and the children ran down stairs to meet their parents. As Mrs. Foster was carried back to her room, she lifted up her veil, and when Eveline saw her kind, sweet face, she did not wonder that Comfort loved her so dearly. Mary looked away, for she was ashamed of herself and displeased with every one else.

Mrs. Davis did not enter the house, but sent for the children to come out to her, so Mary bade Comfort a hasty good-bye, and Eveline an affectionate one, and then they all drove back to Granville.

15

CHAPTER IX.

ONE morning, in the latter part of October, after her father had gone to town, Comfort was almost sure that she heard Fanny making up a fire in the parlor. She ran to see if her ears had not deceived her, but no, there were the blazing hickory logs, making the whole apartment look cheerful.

On asking what was going to happen, the little girl was told that her father had ordered the fire, and wanted the room put in order, because Mrs. Foster was coming down stairs in the middle of the day. Comfort was running up, immediately, to express her delight at this information, to her mother, but the nurse stopped her, saying that her mistress was taking another nap, so as to feel strong enough for the exertion. Comfort then wanted to know if she could not do something to get the room ready, and Fanny gave her a hawk's wing, which she used for a duster, to brush off the chairs and table. A few moments afterwards a wagon stopped at the door, and three men came in the yard, carrying a very pretty couch which Fanny told them they were to set down in the parlor. Then they went back to the wagon for a large stuffed rocking-chair, which they placed before the cheerful fire, and again returned with a great flat box, which was placed in the hall without being opened. Fanny thought that this was the last thing to come in, and was shutting the front door after the men, when one of them came back with a little low chair, just like the larger one, which Comfort was sure was meant for herself, so she had it put close to the one that she knew was for her mother.

It seemed as if wonders were never to cease, that morning, for the wagon had hardly driven away before the little girl saw her father coming in the gate with a plain looking man who had a small round parcel in his hand. Both came right into the parlor, and then Mr. Foster pointed to the harp and said, "There is the instrument; put it in as good order as you can," and the stranger undid the package, and took out a roll of wires, of different sizes, and began comparing them with the harp-strings which were broken. Comfort stood looking on with much interest while this was going forward, and was delighted with the sound when the instrument was tuned.

"Now," said her father, after telling

Fanny where the couch was to be placed, "run and get me a hammer, and you shall see what is in that box, my little daughter."

The hammer was brought in an instant, and then Mr. Foster opened the box and took out two large engravings, which were prettily framed. Comfort thought that she had never seen such pretty pictures, and could hardly admire them enough. One represented the resurrection of our Saviour, and the angels were standing by His empty tomb, while He was pictured as just speaking to Mary. Comfort felt as if she almost heard Him calling her name, and she thought the words under the picture would be so comforting to her mother, for they were, " Even so, them that sleep in Jesus will God bring with Him."

The other picture represented a Christian family as just risen from the tomb,

15*

and about to be caught up in the clouds. Comfort did not know whether she liked the faces of the children, or the cherubs who were waiting to receive them, best, and she thought that all of them looked as if they might be her lost sisters. She admired equally the inscription, which was, "Here am I and the children that God has given me."

When these pictures were unpacked, and his little daughter had looked at them as long as she wished, Mr. Foster went into the parlor, and standing up in a high chair, took down the piece of needlework over the fire place, which Comfort had always so much admired. She wondered why he did this, but his face was so sad as he looked at the broken rose-buds on the tomb-stone, that she did not like to ask any questions. He hung one of the other pictures in its place, and the mate to it over the table opposite, and then carried that which he **had** taken down up into the garret, and put it into **the** flat box which Fanny brought up from the hall. Comfort followed **her** father thither, and sat by while he unpacked some books which she had never seen before, and he let her take two or three little ones down stairs, while he carried several that were larger, and put them on the empty table. This gave the room quite an inhabited air, and both Mr. Foster and Comfort looked round it with great satisfaction.

"Don't you think it wants some flowers?" said Comfort, or, rather, she made signs to that effect. Her father bowed, and the little girl went out in the yard to collect some of the few blossoms that remained, but the only ones that suited her were two roses with a bud between them, and these she placed in a wine-glass on the table, and said they were her father and mother and herself. Then she gathered some large, bright-colored leaves and tall grasses, and made them into bunches which she asked her father to put in the old china vases on each side of the mantel-piece, and now she thought the room was perfectly beautiful.

Mr. Foster had hardly done admiring his morning's work when Fanny came to say that her mistress was ready to come down. He went up stairs directly, and taking her little delicate form in his arms, carried her down into the parlor as easily as if she had been a baby, and seated her in the comfortable rocking-chair.

Comfort drew her little chair close up to her mother's side, and took her hand in both her own, but said nothing, for something told her that it was best to be silent.

After looking around the room with

a pleased, surprised air, Mrs. Foster lifted
her eyes to the place where her last work
was accustomed to hang, and as she saw
the picture which had replaced it, and
read the words, "Even so, them that
sleep in Jesus shall God bring with
Him," her eyes filled with tears. Still,
she did not look unhappy as she turned
to her husband, who stood beside her
chair, and said,

"It is better to look at the resurrection
than the tomb; I have one rose-bud left."

Comfort understood, then, why her
father had made the change, and she
was glad that he thought of it. She
wished that Mary Davis could see her
mother, as she sat there, for she thought
that Mary could not help owning that
she was the sweetest-looking lady in the
world.

After a little while, Mrs. Foster was
tired, so she lay down on the couch,

which she said was very easy and comfortable, and then the little girl drew her chair up to it, and taking out her Testament, read the Lesson for the day, as she was accustomed to do in her mother's chamber. When she had done, Mrs. Foster beckoned to her husband to come to her, and wrote on his hand for some minutes, and then he went out of the room. When he came back, he brought a little bureau, which Comfort had never seen, and which appeared as if it were intended for a doll. His eyes looked as if he had been shedding tears, but he tried to speak cheerfully, as he said,—

"Here it is, my love; are you sure that you are quite strong enough to open it?"

Mrs. Foster replied, that she did not think it would overcome her now, and then she took the key, and unlocking the upper drawer, took out a little picture-book that had once been Harry's, and a paper containing a curl of his hair, which was just the color of Comfort's. The bereaved mother was not as strong as she thought, for the moment that she touched these mementoes, the tears gushed to her eyes, and she trembled all over.

Comfort smoothed her hair gently, and then said, in a low, sweet voice,—

"Mama, would it make you feel badly to see the rattle-box that I had when I was a baby?"

Mrs. Foster was surprised at the question.

"No, my child," she answered, sadly.

"Well, mama," continued Comfort, "do you think Harry and Kate want these things any more now, than I do my rattle-box. If they have plenty of pretty things in heaven, what makes you cry when you look at what they have left behind them?"

The simple reasoning of the child, and the remembrance of the treasure that she had left, consoled the mourner, and she said, fondly,—

"You are a comfort indeed! why should I weep when I see these trifles?"

She then opened the next drawer, and took from it a little cap which was very yellow from having lain there so long.

"This," she said, "was what my little Susan wore the day that she was christened. She exchanged it, an hour afterwards, for an angel's crown. You have never heard me speak much of her, for she was only six weeks old when she was taken from me, and that was my last affliction."

Comfort took the cap on her little hand and tried to imagine the face that had looked out from under it, but she could only see that of the baby in the picture of the risen Christian family.

"These little cups," said Mrs. Foster, handing her daughter two silver cups like her own, " were given to Harry and Kate when they were three years old."

Comfort read the names engraved upon them, and wondered to herself how any one could value such things highly, when they might so soon have to leave them.

The last thing that Mrs. Foster took out of the bureau, was a little box, containing a child's ring, with one pearl set in it.

"This," she said, "was given to Mary by your aunt, but she never lived to wear it. Try it on and see if it is large enough for you."

Comfort found that the ring fitted her, but she felt no wish to wear it till her mother said,—

"Keep it, my dear, and when you look at it, remember always to whom it belonged, and what is necessary to pre-

16

pare you to rejoin your brothers and sisters in heaven. You must take it off when you wash your hands, or the pearl will become dim, and as you do so, think how much care is also necessary lest your soul should likewise grow impure."

Then Comfort pressed the ring to her lips, and promised never to forget why she wore it.

Mrs. Foster now locked up the bureau again, and her husband carried it back to the large trunk in the spare room, where it had been kept for so many years.

CHAPTER X.

IN a few weeks, Mrs. Foster was able to go all around the house, which speedily changed its appearance. The dining-room became really pleasant, and Comfort enjoyed every meal, because her mother was able to sit at the table, and the cook was now a nice, tidy woman, with her kitchen as neat as herself.

The crib in which Comfort had slept ever since she was a baby, was now quite too small for her, and Mrs. Foster asked her little daughter whether she would feel afraid to sleep in a room by herself. Comfort looked surprised at the question from her mama, who had always taught her that there was nothing in the world but sin which ought to be feared. "I did not mean to ask whether you would be afraid, exactly, but I thought perhaps you might be lonely at night," said her mother, in reply to the inquiring glance of the child. The troubled expression passed away from Comfort's face, and she replied, " Oh, no, mama. You know I never speak after I have gone to bed for the night, now, and I think I shall like to feel that I am quite alone with my heavenly Father. I know that He will not let anything hurt me."

Mrs. Foster did not feel easy to have her little girl out of her sight, but the room in which she thought of placing her was between her own and that occupied by Fanny, and the walls were so thin that the least noise could be heard through them, so that she would really be as safe as if she were in her chamber.

The kind mother took a great deal of pleasure in fitting up this little apartment to please Comfort, who had shown, from her infancy, a great love of order. A shade, with a pretty boquet of flowers painted upon it, was placed at the only window, and Mr. Foster bought a light bedstead, to stand in one corner, for which Fanny made a neat white spread, and the toilet was covered with the same material. There were only three chairs in the room, and one of them was a small one, but Comfort said as long as she had a seat for her father and mother it was no matter, and that if she ever had any more company, her bed would do for a sofa. Beside the white toilet, there was another table in the room, and on this stood a little writing desk, which was one of Comfort's greatest treasures. It had been her sister Kate's, and her mother had given it to her on the day when she was seven years old. It was not an expensive one, but very convenient, and beside

16*

it there lay two blank books with which her father had presented her at the same time. One of these was a journal book in which she wrote every day, and in the other she put down the texts from the morning lessons which she most wished to impress upon her mind. Her hand-writing was hardly formed, and the letters were large and irregular, but there was not a blot in either of these books, although she did not show them even to her mother. Many faults were mentioned in the journal to which we have not alluded, for Comfort knew her own heart, and the actions which appeared so right and easy to perform, often cost a struggle within.

When Comfort first took possession of her new room, she had some very solemn thoughts. Beside that bed she was to present her morning and evening petitions to her heavenly Father, and every night to lay down to sleep watched only by His untiring eye. She was a little girl now, but every year would bring new duties, and who knew what would take place in that room? How sweet and comfortable it looked! Was she grateful enough to her kind parents, and to Him who had put it in their hearts to love her so dearly? How could she make them more happy? Perhaps she might go from this little room to that home to which she looked forward with pleasure. Would the angel come thither to call her to the skies? These were deep thoughts for such a little girl, but Comfort had drunk from the fountain of all wisdom. She sought God early, and she found Him. Living always in His presence, her mind outgrew her years, and, while most childlike in manners, her thoughts were often those of a much riper age. She now

knelt by her bed with the same simple
faith that she had always felt in her
merciful Creator, and asked His aid that
she might not think, say, or do anything
in that room which could be displeas-
ing to Him. Then she went into her
mother's chamber to undress, and her
recent serious thoughts gave such peculiar earnestness to her young face,
that her mother felt a sudden dread lest
her darling was ripening for the skies.
She kissed her with unusual tenderness,
and long after the little girl was asleep,
a fond face was bending over her, to be
sure that all was right.

But, although Mrs. Foster was able to
go about the house, which was thoroughly
warmed during the winter by a large
stove in the hall, she did not dare to
venture out till the cold weather was
over. Comfort took a long walk, every
day, with Fanny, and when the snow

came, she would rub it on her cheeks till they blushed like roses.

"Mama," she said, one day, "I read the text, this morning, 'He giveth His snow like wool,' and I have just thought what it means. Does it not keep the earth warm, just as the wool does the sheep who wear it? How good it is in God to give the poor naked ground such a nice white coat! I would like to see the evergreens at Mrs. Davis' to-day, for she told me they were so pretty when they were covered with snow."

Just as Comfort uttered this wish, there was a merry sound of sleigh-bells in the distance, and very soon a sleigh with two swift horses came dashing up to the door.

"Oh, mama, mama," exclaimed Comfort, who was looking out the parlor window, "it is Eveline! oh, I am so glad."

The little girl ran to the door, but she could not reach the knob, so she had to go and call Fanny to let Mrs. Davis and her daughter into the hall. They were all bundled up in cloaks and furs, and did not like to go into the parlor for fear that their cold garments might chill Mrs. Foster, who was still delicate, but they wanted Comfort to ask her mother if she might go with them and take a short sleigh-ride.

The child was so delighted that she could hardly get the words out, and her mother said yes, immediately, and told her to go and get Fanny to wrap her up warm. Mrs. Davis said there were plenty of buffaloes, but Comfort did not know what they were, and she asked Fanny to bring her mother's cloak out to the sleigh and wrap it round her, over the gray pelisse.

"You will want something warmer

over your head, than that hat," said Eveline. "See! I have a scarf tied under my hood."

"I have not any other hat," said Comfort, "but perhaps mama will let me take her long scarf and tie it all round my head." She ran back into the parlor to ask if she might take the scarf, which was a bright red one, that her father had brought to his wife at Christmas. Mrs. Foster told her that she was glad that she had thought of it, and that she had better put on a pair of her gloves over her own little woolen ones. As she was not used to wading in such deep snow, and had no Polish boots like those which Mrs. Davis and Eveline wore, Fanny carried her in her arms through the yard to the sleigh, where she found not only Mary Davis, but Etta Alston and Anna Lathrop. Mrs. Davis would not ask Jane Campbell to join the sleighing party, because she was so disgusted with her manners on the day that she was at Eveline's fête, that she made up her mind that that should be the last invitation she should ever receive to her house.

Mary Davis did not greet the new comer very warmly, but the other little girls were delighted to see her, and Mrs. Davis told her to sit in the back seat, between Eveline and herself. When they were all comfortably settled, the horses started and away they went, at a rate that at first made Comfort quite giddy. She soon got used to the motion and then it was delightful. The whole earth looked so pure, that the child felt as if she had been newly created, and when they came to a wood of evergreens all frosted with snow, she could hardly express her admiration.

"Oh, what a beautiful white dress the

trees have on!" she exclaimed, "and they caught it coming down from heaven. And oh! look at the icicles hanging from those branches; how they sparkle! I know that God can do everything, but do you see, Mrs. Davis, how he could make anything more beautiful?"

"I certainly cannot imagine a more lovely day," said Mrs. Davis, but as she looked at the animated face that peeped out from the folds of the red scarf, she thought that the most beautiful sight in this world was an earnest, affectionate child, adoring the Giver of life, and of all good gifts.

"Oh, I have wanted to see you much," whispered Eveline; "I could not tell you half I wished in my notes, for it takes me so long to write. Mama would not bring me to see you because she thought that Mary did not behave well when we were last here, and we always go out

17

together. I am not afraid to sleep alone now."

Comfort grasped the hand of her companion, and looked up in her face, with a countenance radiant with joy.

"I knew it would be so," she said; "you asked for what I told you, didn't you, dear Eveline?"

"Yes," said the child, bashfully, for she was talking about something which she did not wish any one else to hear.

"So did I," said Comfort, who never imagined that there was any reason why people wished not to be heard when they were speaking of the most important of all subjects.

"What did you do?" asked Mrs. Davis, who was struck with the pleased expression of her little companion.

"I asked that Eveline might have a pure heart," said Comfort, in a low, sweet voice.

Mrs. Davis could not speak for a moment, for her voice was choked by tears. "God bless you, my child," she said, at last, "He heard your prayer, and is making my darling Eveline all I could wish."

CHAPTER XI.

THE winter and spring had passed away, and a beautiful Sunday in June was drawing to a close. Mrs. Foster—now perfectly well—stood at an open window, watching Comfort, who was gathering some roses, while her father walked up and down the path leading to the gate, looking at the various flowers which adorned the once desolate yard. No passer-by now thought it was a gloomy place, for, although the tall brick house was still narrow and stiff, it had been newly painted, and luxuriant vines half concealed its ugliness.

"Mama," said Comfort, as she handed her a boquet of beautiful roses, "won't you please come and take a walk. We shall have time to go to the wood behind the house, before sunset, and I know pàpa would like it."

Mrs. Foster readily consented to do what her darling wished, and then Comfort ran for a sunbonnet and shawl for her mother, and another for herself, although she carried her own on her arm.

Mr. Foster thought it was a very pleasant time for a walk, so he gave his arm to his wife, and they passed through the gate, with Comfort at their side. But when they came to the path which led to the wood, the little girl ran on before her parents, for she felt that there might be some things which they would like to say to each other. A week before, Mr. Foster had been baptized, and his daughter thought it strange that her father should become

17*

so like a little child, but she was glad, for she knew that of such was the king-dom of heaven. On the afternoon of the same day he had been confirmed, and when the Bishop laid his hands upon that dear head, Comfort could hardly breathe, and her lips followed every word of the prayer, "Defend, O Lord, this thy servant with thy heav-enly grace; that he may continue thine for ever; and daily increase in thy Holy Spirit more and more, until he come unto thine everlasting kingdom."

Although the day of her father's con-firmation had been very solemn to Com-fort, that which was now closing was still more interesting, for she had seen both her parents kneeling side by side to receive the holy sacrament. The little girl had often read the account of the Last Supper of our Lord, and how He distributed the bread and wine to

His disciples, saying, "Do this in remembrance of me," and now she wished
that she were old enough to fulfil the
parting command of her dying Saviour.
As the clergyman went from one to the
other of the communicants, she closed
her eyes, and imagined that Christ Himself was passing about among His disciples, speaking those words of love,
"This is my body which was given for
you." She felt as if something was
going on between Jesus and His Church
which was too sacred to be gazed upon,
and involuntarily turned away her eyes
from those who were retiring from the
chancel. When her father and mother
came back to the pew, she quietly left
room for the latter to pass to her seat,
and, young as she was, she could understand why her mother's eyes were filled
with tears. The same quick sense of
delicacy now made her keep in advance

of her parents, for she felt that there were sweet thoughts which they might wish to enjoy together, after their first communion.

The sun was sinking behind the hills, and as Comfort watched the golden glow in the west, she thought that such might be the appearance of that world which would need no sun, because the Lord God would be the light thereof. Earth was daily becoming more pleasant to the Christian child, but it did not withdraw her heart from heaven. Every new source of happiness only made her more sure that perfect joy was laid up in store for those who should be for ever with the Lord. When she saw her mother's health improving, she thought of the time when they should both dwell in that blest home "whose inhabitants shall no more say, I am sick," and the friendship of Eveline gave her sweet anticipation of the pleasure that she should find in the society of her sainted sisters. Every flower that she plucked on earth was an emblem of the immortal ones that she should here-after gather in heavenly fields, and was sweeter for the association.

And so Comfort walked on, with her unseen Saviour at her side, and her heart filled with peace. When she reached the brow of the hill which her father and mother were ascending, she looked around for a seat, and having found the moss-covered trunk of a tree, she threw over it the shawl that she had been carrying on her arm.

"Here, mama," she said, "is a place for you, and one for father close by it. I can sit down at your feet."

Mrs. Foster took the offered seat, but her husband said, "It will not do for you to sit there, my darling; the ground may be damp. I can hold you, though you are getting to be quite a large girl."

Comfort gladly placed herself on her father's knee, and after they had all admired the sweet sunset sky, she said, "Oh, would it not be nice to have evening prayers here. Father, haven't you got your Bible with you? I saw you put it in your pocket when we came out of church."

"Yes, my love," he replied, "and if your mother will first sing a hymn, I will read a chapter in it."

Mrs. Foster immediately commenced those sweet words,

> " Softly now the light of day
> Fades upon my sight away,"

in which Comfort joined with much taste and feeling. Mr. Foster could not hear the pleasant voices of his wife and child, but he was making melody in his heart, and thinking of the time when his ear should be unstopped, and he could unite in the songs of heaven.

As the music died away in the distance, Mr. Foster took a small Bible out of his pocket, and opening to the Old Testament, read the history of Naaman the Syrian.

Comfort had often heard the story before, but to-night it seemed particularly interesting, for her father appeared to feel every word that he read. When he had finished the chapter, he laid his hand on his daughter's head, and asked, with peculiar emphasis, "Do you not think, my love, that it was very kind in the little maiden to feel so much anxiety for the welfare of Naaman?"

"Not so very," replied Comfort, "for if she knew who could cure him, how could she help telling him?"

"But," asked Mr. Foster, in the same

earnest tone, "do you not think that she must have been very happy to know that she had been the means of doing so much good?"

"Oh, yes, indeed," replied Comfort, warmly, but she could not understand why her father asked her a question of this kind.

"But suppose," continued Mr. Foster, "that Naaman had been her father instead of her master, would she not then have had reason for great thankfulness?"

A sudden perception of her father's meaning now glanced through Comfort's mind, and her blue eyes were fixed with tearful earnestness upon his face, while he said, "My beloved child, do you remember the evening when you sat thus upon my knee, and pointed at the picture of Samuel and of Jacob, and then gave me a look of such affectionate entreaty? I was the leper then, Comfort, and you were the little maiden who pointed out to me the great Physician."

Comfort could not speak, but she clasped both arms around her father's neck and kissed him tenderly, and then she laid her young, fair head upon his bosom, and, closing her eyes, thanked her heavenly Father for his unspeakable mercy.

Mrs. Foster looked at the pure, sweet face of her child, as she was thus employed, with unutterable love, and laid her trembling hand upon her husband's arm with a look which said, "God has blessed us indeed." He took that hand in his own and replied, tenderly, "I am deeply indebted to your untiring devotion and constant prayers, but next to you, under God, I owe my salvation to the earnest faith and sweet example of our dear little Comfort."